"I'm tired of this charade you call marriage."

Kirk's reaction was immediate, and his air of indifference hurt her.

"As you remember," he said, "you agreed to act the part of my wife until the contract I need is secured."

"And then what makes you expect I'll go on living here?"

"Well, for one thing, your business is a flop. And for another, you'll never form a lasting relationship with any man as long as you're still emotionally tied to a ghost."

Now Imogen was furious. "Who are you to judge me? And how can you possibly class my cosmetic line as a failure? Contrary to what you seem to think, I'm not completely incompetent."

"If you were completely incompetent," replied Kirk, his words clipped and impersonal, "I'd have washed my hands of you long before this."

JENNY ARDEN, a British writer, combines a career as a college lecturer in business studies with the writing she has always wanted to do. Her favorite place for relaxation is North Wales, but travel fascinates her—both the places she has visited and the places she dreams about for future journeying. In her spare time she enjoys sculpting historical figures in clay and cooking for company. Huckleberry, her Burmese Blue cat, is her companion while writing. He usually sits in a chair beside the typewriter, but occasionally in a fit of jealousy, will bid for her attention by sitting on the keys! This is Jenny's first book in the Harlequin Presents line.

JENNY ARDEN

to the victor, the spoils

Harlequin Books

TORONTO • NEW YORK • LONDON
AMSTERDAM • PARIS • SYDNEY • HAMBURG
STOCKHOLM • ATHENS • TOKYO • MILAN

Harlequin Presents first edition April 1988
ISBN 0-373-11063-4

Original hardcover edition published in 1987
by Mills & Boon Limited

CHAPTER ONE

'IMOGEN, Mr Cameron's here.'

Imogen glanced up sharply from the bank balances she had been studying, the anxiety in her eyes deepening into startled alarm. She hadn't been expecting Kirk till one. It was only just gone twelve. She realised now just how much she had been relying on that time to brace herself for seeing him again.

Gathering up the papers she had been working with, she said with a convincing semblance of calm,

'Thank you, Tracey. Tell him I'll be with him right away.'

Tracey nodded and went out of the office door, her efficient walk emphasised by her trimly fitting uniform.

Without pausing to put the papers in order, Imogen hurriedly slipped them into the top drawer of her desk. She'd resume worrying about the financial state of the company later. Right now she could only think about Kirk and how to handle a meeting that was going to be difficult for both of them, but especially for her.

She remembered the faint curiosity in Tracey's eyes as she had informed her that Kirk had arrived. Tracey had started work as one of the beauticians at New Radiance's main salon a month ago. She obviously didn't know the set-up, only enough to assume that her employer was divorced. It was a natural enough assumption, except that Imogen wasn't divorced from Kirk, not yet. That was why she had asked to see him. She had been separated from him for almost a year. Now she wanted to make that separation final.

Imogen went out of her office into the jacuzzi area of

the beauty salon. A domed, tinted-glass roof let in an abundance of sunlight which fell brightly on the Italian-tiled floor. The water in the jacuzzi foamed gently, sending up thin wisps of steam. The faint fragrance of cosmetics added to the serenity created by the sound of swirling water, lavish sunlight and Mediterranean-style décor.

Normally Imogen walked past the full-length mirror on her way through to the hairdressing salon and reception area without a glance. But not today. Knowing that she looked the part of the successful business woman was reassuring. It wasn't just that she wanted to meet Kirk as his equal, as someone who belonged to the hard, swift-moving business world as much as he did. It was also that she had no intention of allowing him the least suspicion that he'd been right when he'd predicted that New Radiance Limited would be trading insolvent within the year if she didn't take some action.

Her suit, with its bold blouson jacket and severe, straight skirt, emphasised her athletic slimness. She was slightly above average height. Dark blonde hair, cut into an attractively tousled shoulder-length style, framed a face with grey eyes fringed with blonde-tipped lashes. Usually she looked as though she smiled readily, but now, with her hands slipped into the pockets of her jacket, and her eyes slightly wary, she seemed tense and already on the defensive.

She turned away from the mirror and taking a steadying breath, she walked through into reception, her heels tapping smartly, her shoulders imperceptibly squared.

The reception desk was in the front of the hairdressing salon, screened from the gold-tinted plate glass by a display of pot plants. Kirk was sitting on the banquette that lined the wall. He was glancing through one of the trade journals without apparent interest.

In his mid-thirties, he had a hard, wide-shouldered

build. The jacket of his expensively tailored suit was undone. The casual relaxation of his body made his lean, agile strength more disturbing. His eyes were dark with flecks of attractive grey light in them, eyes that were astute and direct. He had dark hair, the swarthy skin of a buccaneer and a firm yet faintly humorous mouth.

Imogen remembered how, until she had got to know him, she had found his unshakeable self-possession a shade unnerving. Now, with nothing but coldness between them, there was still something a mite intimidating about his careless assurance.

She reminded herself that she was on view to both her staff and customers. This was no time to let it be obvious that she did not feel entirely in control of either her emotions or the situation. She hadn't expected that seeing Kirk again would produce such a confused inner response on her part. In the year they had been apart she had convinced herself that she no longer loved him. Already the pain she felt on seeing him was making inroads on that certainty. She couldn't afford to give in to speculation. She reminded herself that her feelings for him were dead. They had to be.

He glanced up, hearing her approach, and she was conscious of his dark eyes assessing her, studying her without any pretence that he was doing otherwise. They might have been two people who had only ever known each other in the most casual sort of way. A curious chill sense of loneliness tugged at her heart, which she fought against impatiently. When a relationship was over, that was the end of it. There was no point in trying to sustain it with pretence. She had been right to walk out on Kirk, just as she was right now in wanting a divorce.

Kirk set the magazine aside and stood up.

'Tuesday seemes to have a kind of significance where we're concerned,' he remarked, his voice a shade dry.

'It was a Tuesday that you packed your things and left.'

'Was it?' she said, lifting her chin slightly as she met his gaze. 'I don't remember.'

She had intended to sound merely indifferent, but her comment came across as more unfeeling than that. Kirk gave a brief smile that had little humour in it and then said,

'Well, anyway, it's good to see you again.'

His words were a formality, so she was not prepared for his taking hold of her gently by the arm as he bent to kiss her on the cheek. She caught her breath slightly at the unexpected physical contact. She had a brief impression of his dominating height, the roughness of his face against hers, the brush of his lips before he released her, though her senses still seemed to record in memory the imprint of his touch. Her response to him aggravated her, making her formerly confused feelings towards him harden into hostile dislike.

With a curious mixture of heightened colour and coldness of voice, she said, deliberately passing up his remark,

'We may as well get going. I don't want to be out of the shop long.'

'Why is that?' he asked carelessly. 'Aren't things going too well?'

'Everything's just fine,' Imogen said, a shade too resentfully for conviction. 'As I told you it would be.'

Kirk glanced at her sceptically before saying, his firm voice tinged with sarcasm,

'And if things weren't so good, of course, you'd tell me.'

Imogen didn't answer him. Her eyes met his briefly in mute hostility. Somehow, already, he had taken charge of the conversation, forcing her on to the defensive. This wasn't the way she had planned it. But then it wasn't easy putting up a strong façade when things were going so badly for her. Pride, in part, had made her walk out on him.

That same fierce pride demanded that he shouldn't know now just how close New Radiance was to going into compulsory liquidation. The insecurity she had lived with for the past few months about the state of the company made her vulnerable.

'I thought we'd have lunch at the White Hart,' Imogen said, refusing to be drawn by his comment.

'When I got your message I booked a table at the Folie à Deux,' Kirk told her.

'Well, I wish you hadn't,' said Imogen, a shade curtly.

If she'd meant anything to him, she thought, with a stab of pain, he couldn't have chosen that particular restaurant. To be reminded of how little he felt for her was salutary. It made it easier for her to harden her feelings towards him into chill animosity.

'Why?' asked kirk, his eyes cool and observant as he looked at her. 'You used to like the place.'

'That was before we split up. There's no point raking up memories.'

'Were they such bad times to look back on?' he asked, a slight edge to his voice as, together, they left the salon.

'If they weren't, we'd still be together,' Imogen replied briefly. 'We're not, so I suppose that answers the question.'

She saw his jawline harden a little and knew, with a curious sense of redress, that she had succeeded in hitting back. The feeling was followed swiftly by a twist of dismay. Once they had been close. Now a gulf of animosity separated them. She hadn't meant to remember the good times between them. It hurt too much. It was strange that it should when she accepted that their marriage was over.

She wished suddenly that she hadn't decided on this meeting. She should have contacted him solely through her solicitor. That way she could have retained the wall of indifference to him she had carefully built up, without the fear that it wasn't as substantial as she had supposed and that, if he meant to, he could smash it.

Kirk had parked his Mercedes on the shop's forecourt. She realised it had been a further mistake to suggest that he meet her at the salon. She should have arranged for them to meet at the White Hart. Then she would have arrived in her own car and been on neutral territory.

Kirk opened the passenger door for her and she got in. He started the ignition and pulled out on to the main road. Imogen was conscious of the constrained silence between them. Light conversation seemed out of place in view of what their meeting was leading up to.

As she searched for something to say, Kirk asked, 'I take it you haven't had a break from the business so far this year?'

'I'm taking a holiday later on,' Imogen said convincingly, if a shade evasively.

With the precarious state of the company, she couldn't contemplate a break. She hoped her answer struck the right note of carelessness.

Kirk's eyes flickered to her as he commented,

'You look as if you could do with a holiday. You were always slim, but you've lost weight.'

'I'm in the beauty business,' Imogen reminded him. 'I have to watch my weight.'

He gave her a deliberate, sceptical glance that challenged her convenient explanation. She had never been able to hide from his shrewd perceptiveness. When things had been good between them, it had seemed part of the bond of pairing. Now it made her feel on edge. Sparring with Kirk was like arguing with an opponent who had the advantage of knowing exactly where to test her shaky defences.

There was a short silence and then Kirk asked, his eyes intent on the road,

'Why don't you level with me?'

'Level with you about what?' she asked sharply, braced for a spirited denial that anything was wrong with the business.

'You don't need it spelt out,' he said. 'You know perfectly well what I'm talking about. New Radiance was in trouble before we split up. In so far as your brother's still the Finance Director, I imagine it's been going downhill pretty fast since then. What I want to know is how bad things are.'

'You can leave Jim out of this,' Imogen said fiercely. 'And as it so happens, you're wrong about the business. Stick to giving advice to the companies you audit the accounts for. You're not on my payroll and I can do without your recommendations.'

She'd over-reacted. Her act of the prosperous business woman who didn't need his help either financially or as an emotional back-up now showed too clearly as a sham. She hadn't wanted to give him the satisfaction of knowing his judgement had been correct. He'd advised her to buy Jim out because he was too much of a liability, and she'd refused to listen.

'Then you didn't ask to see me because you wanted to arrange a loan,' he said.

The insult of his comment was so intense that she suddenly hated him for his ability always to hold all the aces. She was tired of having the losing script.

'I wouldn't ask you for a loan to get me out of a debtors' prison,' she said contemptuously.

'Fortunately, debtors' prisons no longer exist,' Kirk reminded her before adding drily, 'but I get the general idea.'

For a while, neither of them spoke. The silence between them seemed to be emphasised by the smooth running sound of the car engine. The London suburbs were giving way to green-belt land. The summer heat that had seemed oppressive in the urban streets made the countryside indolent and replete. The grass by the roadside that had gone up tall was as scorched and golden as the hazy fields of corn.

The Folie à Deux was an old coaching inn situated in one of the larger Chiltern villages. Its white frontage was turned to brilliance by the bright sunlight. An archway led into a cobbled courtyard.

Kirk parked the car and together they went into the restaurant. If he had heartlessly chosen the Folie à Deux to remind her of the past he couldn't have picked a better venue. To ward them off, Imogen rekindled the rather disjointed conversation they had kept up in the car.

'Do you spend much time in Gloucestershire these days?'

'I haven't spent a weekend at our cottage since we had Stephen and Miriam staying with us that time. In fact, I was thinking of putting it on the market. Maybe that's something we could get sorted out. Of course, I won't sell it if you still want to use it as a weekend getaway.'

'No, I shan't do that.'

Kirk had inherited the cottage from his aunt. It was too much his property for her to have thought of using it during the time of their separation. Whether he wanted to sell it or not was completely his affair.

They went into the restaurant, Kirk ducking slightly under the low lintel. The waiter showed them to a table that was pleasantly secluded. The simple table-settings and the quiet, unhurried service had made the restaurant one of Imogen's favourites. She and Kirk had had dinner here on their first wedding anniversary. It was ironic that their relationship should end here too.

Kirk ordered and then turned to her to pick up on their conversation.

'You're very welcome to use the cottage any weekend,' he told her. 'You needn't worry that you're going to run into me, though even if I was there, the cottage does have three bedrooms.'

His implication was obvious. Just the idea of being alone with him again, sharing the rather isolated cottage as an echo of the intimacy of marriage, was strangely disturbing.

'I can't spare the time to get away right now even if I wanted to,' she said, before adding, 'Look, you don't have to be concerned about me. I don't need a rest from work. I'm fine.'

She felt the probe of his dark eyes, but refused to meet their steely directness.

'And why shouldn't I still be concerned about you?' Kirk asked, his resolute voice a shade harsh. 'After all, you *are* still my wife.'

'It's a little late to be playing the part of the caring husband now,' Imogen said derisively. 'You're not really interested in me. I'm just one of your assets. The only reason you married me was because you felt it was advantageous to you.'

'And what were your motives?' he asked in a voice that bit with sarcasm.

Imogen coloured a little and said with quiet defiance,

'You knew I wasn't in love with you when I married you. There was never any pretence. I was fool enough to think that we got on well enough together for that not to matter. And maybe it wouldn't have if you hadn't started working with Lydia Slater. Except you weren't just working together, were you? Your relationship went a lot deeper than that.'

'So we're back to Lydia,' Kirk said impatiently.

'Yes, we are,' Imogen countered fiercely, keeping her voice low so that he wouldn't hear the emotion in it.

Why wasn't she handling this better? She had meant to be calm, reasonable, detached, and instead she was so close to tears that angry resentment was the only way to fight them back. She had thought she had learned to accept the fact that he was involved with another woman. But now the same feelings of betrayal and hurt anger were welling up, making her hate him for having the power to destroy so utterly her inner calm.

'I wasn't settling for a complete sham of a marriage,' she continued bitterly.

She broke off as the manager stopped by at their table to enquire pleasantly if they were enjoying their meal.

'Nice to see you again, Mr Cameron.' He nodded politely at Imogen. 'Mrs Cameron.'

'Your chef's as good as ever. It's hard to keep away,' Kirk said easily.

Imogen looked away, fighting to keep her feelings under control. The contrast between the reality of the situation and the impression she and Kirk gave of being a couple, talking quietly over a leisurely lunch as though reluctant to rush their time together, was cruel enough to hurt.

The manager moved away to the other tables and Kirk reached out to take her hand in his. She started at his touch, her eyes meeting his in mute hostility as he said emphatically,

'There was nothing between Lydia and me, nothing that meant anything.'

'Just how naïve do you think I am?' she countered swiftly, withdrawing her hand, resenting his imprisoning grasp. 'I don't know why you bother to deny it.'

'Because maybe it would make some difference to the way things are right now,' said Kirk, before breaking off with harassed impatience, as though she taxed his endurance.

He was angry and she knew it took a lot of provocation for his temper to be visible.

'You mean a few more lies might help our relationship along?' she said.

She saw his face harden so that his eyes had a dominating steely force as he studied her.

'Did running out help?' he asked with taunting contempt.

'What was I supposed to do?' she countered with another question. 'Close my eyes? Pretend I didn't know what was happening?'

'You could have tried listening,' Kirk suggested, his voice hard. 'I should have been firmer with you from the start.'

'Oh, should you?' she said. 'It seems to me you were quite firm enough. Whatever I wanted to do you were always there to put the veto on it. That's the great joke, isn't it? First there was my father who criticised me for everything. The only thing I ever did that he approved of was my marrying you. But all I did was to swap his criticism for yours.'

She wasn't being fair, but she wasn't stopping to weigh her allegations. Instead she rushed on,

'The trouble was, you never wanted me to continue in business once we were married.'

'I didn't want you in business with that fool of a brother of yours,' Kirk interrupted her. 'I'd have backed you all the way in it if it hadn't been a joint venture. Investing the money your mother left in trust for you in a business with Jim was worse than bad judgement. It was financial suicide.'

'Well, the business hasn't folded yet,' she said curtly.

'This isn't getting us anywhere,' said Kirk, before going on with his usual purposefulness. 'You didn't suggest we meet to ask me for a loan, nor seemingly to try for a reconciliation. So just what is this about?'

He had given her the opening the needed, yet somehow she couldn't immediately find the courage to make the blunt statement that she wanted a divorce. She didn't usually lack resolve. Was it that it was easier to live with the status quo or was she more tied to Kirk than she had realised? No, it couldn't be that. She was through with him. He'd taught her how to love him and she wished with a savage intensity that she'd never learned. How much easier it would have been if she'd retained the illusion that it was Graeme she loved, Graeme—who was dead.

'So?' Kirk asked promptingly, watching her with that steady, considering gaze she found so unsettling.

'I want a divorce,' she said shortly.

CHAPTER TWO

FOR a moment, the silence between them was so acute that it seemed to defeat time. Then Kirk rested an elbow on the table and ran his fingers along his forehead.

When he looked across at her, his face was set hard.

'You've met someone else,' he said, his tone clipped, more as a statement than a question.

'I have been seeing someone else,' Imogen admitted, 'but that's not the reason.'

'Are you sleeping with him?'

The abrupt unexpectedness of the question startled her.

'You've no right to ask me that!' she said angrily, provoked by his double standard of morality.

He reached across the table and caught hold of her arm with a swift violence that made her gasp.

'I've every right to ask you.'

His fingers were bruising her, but she refused to plead to be released. Instead, she said,

'No, I'm not sleeping with Peter, but if I want to, I will, whether I'm still legally married to you or not.'

Kirk let go of her and she went on, furious to find that her voice was noticeably unsteady,

'Our marriage is over. Nothing could ever bring us together again. You don't love me—you never did. Why make this harder than it need be?'

Kirk didn't answer immediately. Then he said harshly,

'This isn't the place for this kind of discussion.'

He signalled to the waiter for the bill and then they

left. In complete silence they walked across the court-yard, Kirk's hand at her elbow, the uncaring hand of a man in authority, forcibly escorting someone on trial. He opened the car door for her and she got in, hoping he couldn't guess at her tremulousness. Now wasn't the time for a display of weakness.

Wordlessly, he started the car. She was acutely aware of his physical nearness, of the substantial width of his shoulders as he drove with the easy skill she had always admired. She rubbed her arm, still feeling the bruising bite of his grip. She remembered the gentleness of his touch on other, intimate occasions.

She had thought she was in love with Graeme, but it was Kirk who had shown her what depths of response she was capable of to a man. She had assumed that Graeme would be the man with whom she would lose her virginity. Instead it had been Kirk, and through their lovemaking she had come to understand that her feelings for him went so very much deeper than her feelings for Graeme ever had. She had thought that the way he touched her and the waves that overpowered her body when he made love to her were responsible for bringing emotional depth to their relationship. She hadn't realised that her response to him was so complete because she was falling in love with him. That love had now cooled, but she couldn't forget the magic he had tapped deep within her.

Kirk glanced at her and then commented, his voice brusque,

'I didn't mean to hurt you.'

'You didn't,' she lied. 'It's just that I bruise easily.'

He smiled briefly, a smile that had nothing to do with mirth. She understood the implication. Physically she might bruise easily, but where emotions were concerned, he thought her somewhere slightly short of callous.

'You don't think we can work things out, then?' he asked, his voice clipped.

It wasn't a question. It was more like a summarising of their relationship, and a bitter one at that.

'Do you?' she returned sceptically.

He didn't answer immediately, and then he said,

'I don't know that I intend letting you go.'

'Why not?' she demanded.

His gaze flickered briefly towards her.

'As you pointed out to me once, I don't like giving up what belongs to me.'

'I'm not your property,' she said fiercely.

'One of my assets was, I think, how you described it,' he reminded her goadingly. 'Before I part with you, I'd like at least to know what your plans are. Do you intend marrying Peter?'

'No,' she said. 'At least, not yet. But my plans have got nothing to do with you. I'm asking for a divorce, not for your consent as to my actions.'

'And where,' Kirk continued, his voice edged with light sarcasm, 'does Graeme fit into all this? How does Peter feel about sharing a cosy *ménage à trois* with a ghost? Or are you over Graeme now?'

It was the first time he had ever spoken to her so brutally about her dead fiancé. The long, ever-tautening strain of the business, coupled with the stress of seeing him again, made her nerves crack abruptly. Tears stung her eyes. She looked down so that Kirk wouldn't see them. She wasn't crying over Graeme, but at least if Kirk sensed her distress he would assume that was the reason.

The narrow country lane opened out just ahead into a passing point and Kirk swung into it.

'Imogen,' he began, 'I shouldn't have said . . . '

She cut across him in a voice that was unsteady with vehemence and emotion. She had loved him and it had meant nothing to him. She had the sudden wish to hurt him as he had hurt her.

'I don't know why I ever married you. I wasn't in love with you, but at least I liked and respected you. Now I loathe you.' She snapped her seat-belt undone and continued, 'And you needn't bother to drive me back to the shop. There's a pub at the next crossroads. I'll phone for a taxi.'

She went to open the door, but he was too quick for her. He caught hold of her by the shoulders, turning her insistently to face him.

'Don't be ridiculous,' he said curtly.

Imogen looked up at him with rebellious eyes that were bright with tears. He was very close to her. His tone had not prepared her for the concern she saw briefly in his face. Then it was gone, and she wondered if she had misread it.

And then, before she could guess his intention, he took her roughly into his arms. In startled protest she pushed her hands against his chest as his lips closed on hers, kissing her with a fierceness and completeness that demanded a response. For an instant she tried to resist, to hold out against the bewildering conflict of emotion that made her suddenly, unreasoningly, want to slide her hands around his neck and press closely to him as her lips parted under his.

A treacherous current of feeling seemed to be running through her, dangerously sensual, destroying all reason, all reality. Her heart was beating so fast she felt shaky, reckless, oblivious of the past. His lips, hard and insistent on her own as he kissed her closely and demandingly, were evoking such a flare-up of longing that, without knowing how it happened, she was suddenly responding with a confessing willingness. Her fingers slid through his thick hair above his collar as she kissed him back, before sanity returned with a rush.

Contempt for herself made her reaction all the more

intense. She pulled away from him, her eyes blazing. Before she could sort out her confused emotions, Kirk demanded with repressed violence,

'Why was it that when Graeme had your soul, he never had your body?'

His grip on her arms tightened as though he was about to force her close to him again. Without conscious thought and partly to protect herself from him, she slapped him full across the face. There was the sharp sound of the blow and, as Kirk released her, she turned away, her eyes dark with dismay. She clenched her hands rigidly so he wouldn't see she was trembling from reaction.

'I'll take you back to the shop,' he said in a voice that was so tightly controlled it half frightened her.

He started the engine. His dark hair had fallen across his forehead and he ran angry fingers through it. His swarthy skin showed only the faintest mark where she had struck him, though she had slapped him with some force. Imogen saw that his face was set hard so that his cheeks looked more hollow, his jawline uncompromising and ruthless.

The tension between them that had shattered momentarily when she had hit him was now more menacingly oppressive. She didn't dare even try to break the silence. She should have anticipated that something like this might happen.

Whatever the flaws in their marriage, for two years she had shared Kirk's life, his thoughts, his bed. Ending such an intimate relationship was bound to be charged with untempered feelings. That alone was enough to account for her reaction. Maybe to some extent it even explained his. Kirk might be self-possessed, purposeful, sardonic even and with few illusions, but he was human as much as she.

More than that, he was too used to forcing events to his will to accept readily that she was instigating the final break-up of their marriage. When Kirk acquired any possession, be it a company asset, or a wife, he didn't relinquish it unless it pleased him to do so. Could she really wonder that, instead of the reasonable, austerely calm discussion she had imagined, their meeting had turned into a sudden explosion of barely repressed violence?

'If it hadn't been for Lydia, would you still be pressing for a divorce?' he asked abruptly, startling her from her thoughts.

'That's a pretty meaningless remark, isn't it?' she said, her voice sharp with animosity. 'Your affair with Lydia wasn't a hypothetical situation. It was a fact.'

He didn't deny it.

There was a short, strained silence and then he commented, his voice hard,

'I didn't realise when you walked out on me it was a prelude to this. If I had, I might not have been so liberal-minded about it.'

'I should have thought . . . ' Imogen began before breaking off.

'You should have thought what?' he asked, before adding derisively, 'Don't tell me you've decided against the comment. You've been pretty forthright up to now.'

He was right. She had reconsidered what she'd been about to say. Her accusations about his infidelity could too easily give the impression that more than just her pride had been damaged. She wouldn't give him the satisfaction of knowing she had once loved him.

'I don't want to fight with you,' she said briefly.

'No,' he agreed sarcastically. 'You want a nice, civilised, modern divorce.'

She didn't answer. They were already nearing the nucleus of shops where the main salon was located. She wanted to get away from him, to escape from this barbed interchange of words. Why couldn't things have worked out differently for them? She didn't want to acknowledge her bitter regrets that their marriage had floundered. Regrets were useless. She tried to push them away, but they were there, making her remember times with him that she hadn't wanted to remember.

He was ten years older than she was and she had married him at twenty-three. He was a business contact of her father's and she had met him shortly after she had become engaged to Graeme. It had been curious, the impression he had made on her. Even that first occasion when he had called at the house to discuss an investment policy with her father had stayed sharply etched in her mind.

Her father had introduced them.

'Imogen, I'd like you to meet Kirk Cameron. If you ever need advice on investment, he's the man.'

His tone was unusually jocular. Whatever the policy Kirk had advised her father to take out, it must be offering a very good return.

There had been something about Kirk's keen-eyed appraisal of her, and the impression he gave of flinty determination, that unsettled her and yet which put her on her mettle in a way that was pleasantly bracing. But Graeme occupied too much space in her life for her to wonder about her reaction to Kirk. Besides, her father approved of him and respected his judgement, and that alone was enough to make her reserved with him. She made polite conversation with him when he stopped by to see her father and their relationship over the next couple of months got no further.

That altered rapidly when the time came that she needed someone to turn to. The day following the news that Graeme had been killed, he had come round to the house. Imogen opened the door to him, enfolded

in a numb stillness that made her look at him blankly
for a moment,

'Hello, Kirk,' she began wanly. 'I'm afraid Dad's
not in yet.'

'I didn't come to see him,' Kirk said, his resolute
voice oddly gentle. 'I've just heard the news about
Graeme. I'm so very sorry.'

She couldn't answer immediately. She had thought
she had wept till she was empty of all tears, but the
concern she saw for her in his dark eyes and his
sincere, unobtrusive sympathy made her throat tighten
suddenly.

'I still can't believe it,' she began in an unsteady
voice. 'I can't believe I'm never going to see him . . . '

She broke off abruptly, covering her face with her
hands as sobs shook her. And then, without quite
knowing how it happened, she was in Kirk's arms,
being held tightly while she gave way to a hopeless
storm of tears. She clung to him, a strange sense of
solace at his strength and protectiveness gradually
steadying her.

At last she made a feeble effort to disengage herself,
fumbling for a handkerchief as she began to apologise
for breaking down. He swept her words aside, keeping
a protective arm round her as he led her into the
drawing-room.

'Believe me,' he said, and his voice held both
authority and kindness, 'it will get easier. You think
right now the pain of grieving is never going to end,
but slowly it will get easier to accept.'

'I loved him so much,' she said brokenly, her voice
anguished.

'I know,' he said simply.

He drew her down on to the sofa and it seemed
natural for her to turn her tear-stained face into his
substantial shoulder. From her father she had had
neither sympathy, nor understanding, and now

suddenly, apart from the engulfing comfort of Kirk's closeness, there was the emotional release of sharing her grief with someone who'd listen.

She was convinced that she would never love any man as she loved Graeme, but her feelings for Kirk in the weeks that followed became steadily more complicated than mere friendship. In the utter loneliness following Graeme's death she needed someone to care about her and someone to care for.

Looking back, she couldn't fully disentangle her reasons for accepting Kirk's proposal that had come too suddenly for her to make sense of her decision. She'd stopped by at his house with some papers her father had signed.

'This saves me a phone call,' said Kirk as he accepted the papers. 'I was going to give you a ring later to ask you to have dinner with me tonight.'

'I'd like that.'

'From the promptness of your answer, dare I hope the papers were an excuse to call?' he said, his eyes gently mocking as he pulled her nearer.

'Maybe,' she conceded with a smile, her heartbeat quickening.

'That's a cautious answer.'

'I know,' she agreed, fighting the flare-up of longing she felt for him with flippancy, 'but I thought a straight yes sounded a little brazen.'

Kirk laughed.

'And what's wrong with being a little brazen?' he asked softly as he bent to kiss her neck.

The brush of his lips against her skin was light, in keeping with their playful conversation.

'Do you know, I could kiss you all over?' he said, raising his head so that his gaze met hers.

His tone hadn't changed, but there was a sudden, searching intensity in his eyes that made the mood between them veer without warning to embered sensuality. She felt a warm rush of colour come into her face. For an instant Graeme came into her mind, and with it a stab of pain and confusion that made her want to lose herself in Kirk's nearness. Her arms went up around his neck as he bent his head to kiss her long and deeply.

She had thought her emotions were so numbed after Graeme's death she would never feel again, but Kirk's touch and the arousing intimacy of his kiss were stirring her with an overwhelming yearning. Her wave of response to him was so fierce it was half frightening, making a twist of emotion catch at her heart.

He was moulding her to his lean, hard body, his kiss tender, yet urgent, leaving no doubt that he wanted her. When at last he raised his head she was trembling.

'You know what I really want?' he said softly. 'Not to take you out to dinner, but to spend the evening seducing you.'

His eyes held hers. She was incapable of answering, swept by a helpless yielding that made her blush more deeply.

He pulled her down on to the sofa, his hand brushing her hair back from her face.

'Kirk,' she began unsteadily, not knowing whether she was protesting or consenting to his making love to her.

'Have I told you how beautiful you are, how much I want to hold you and touch you?' he asked, his voice low.

He bent over her, easing her down on to the cushions as he kissed her with a swift progression from gentleness to possessive desire. She felt his hand cover her breast and she slid her hands over his strong back, hit by a dizzy longing. His fingers deftly undid the buttons of her blouse and she gave a low moan as she felt his warm, arousing touch on her bare skin.

'God, I swear you get me that I don't know what I'm doing,' he said suddenly, as though the words were wrenched from him.

He straightened up, pulling her tightly to him. He held her close while slowly her senses cleared. Then he released her and stood up abruptly. Shakily Imogen started to fasten her blouse. He didn't watch her.

'We'd better get going while I can still stop myself from undressing you,' he said, and though he smiled at her there was a fierce, driving light in his eyes that made her avert her own in confusion.

'We don't have to go out,' she said, her voice low and meaningful.

The invitation of her remark made the silence between them enmeshed in possibilities. She was suddenly aghast at what she'd said. She was offering to sleep with him. She wanted him to make love to her, to take complete possession of her. The knowledge left her perturbed and uncertain. She had chosen not to sleep with Graeme till they were married and till now had never wondered at her restraint.

'Would it help you to forget?' asked Kirk, his voice utterly quiet.

The danger of an instant ago had gone. His comment had shocked her into sanity. She stood up, running a distraught hand through her hair as she said, her voice harrowed,

'I don't know.' She swung round to face him and went on desperately, 'I just want to feel *something*. Most of the time, the time I'm not with you, I'm just hollow inside, as if when Graeme died, something in me died, too.'

She got no further. Kirk crossed the room to her and it seemed right to be enfolded in his arms. He held her for a long time and then he said, his voice calm to the point of coldness,

'Marry me, Imogen.'

She lifted her chin and looked at him in complete bewilderment.

'Did I imagine what you just said?' she managed with a shaky smile.

'No,' he said evenly, moving away from her and making it seem as though the driving passion between them of a moment ago had never happened.

'But why?' she began. 'You know I don't love you.'

'Yes, I know that.' His tone was a shade more clipped. 'But this isn't a love-match I'm suggesting. We've enough in common for a stable marriage, and in my line of work I need a wife who's an asset. You're a warm, intelligent woman, and with your father a diplomat you come from a good background and you're used to playing the hostess. With the entertaining I have to do and the conferences I have to attend you could be very useful to me. I'm sorry if this sounds very practical, but I'm a practical man. I want you for what you can offer me.'

Their conversation was as cool and clear-cut as a business merger, leaving Imogen no possible illusions as to why he was asking her to be his wife. She sat down on the sofa and said, keeping her voice as level as his own,

'Why? You can't need me as a social asset. You've your own firm specialising in management consultancy that has a real name for professionalism, and you've more money than you could possibly ever need. You could . . . '

He cut across her.

'I want a wife with your kind of background. Yes, I've got money now, but I started out in the inner city with a father who walked out on my mother before I was born.'

He paused and she sat quietly, watching his face, sensing intuitively both that what he had begun to tell her was important and that he didn't talk about it readily.

'My father was an aimless no-good who never held down a steady job in his life. I don't know if you can imagine what it's like being brought up with no opportunities and no future. Anyway, my mother died when I was thirteen.' His eyes became a shade more remote, though his voice was as even as before.

He was talking about a past that evoked memories that went deep. It made her feel strangely close to him and she asked quietly,

'How did you manage after that?'

His eyes came back to her, sharply focused, and he said,

'I went to live with my widowed aunt in Gloucestershire. She was very good to me. She was determined I should have as good an education as I could get. It would have helped her if I'd left school at sixteen, but she wouldn't hear of it. When I was studying for my A levels and at university she took on a couple of part-time, low-paid jobs. She always worked too hard.' He drew a deep breath. 'It was a long time before I could make things easier for her. By then, I'd passed my professional exams and I was starting to go up the financial ladder fairly rapidly. Money was no longer a problem.' A smile that was tinged with regret momentarily softened his face. 'At least she had a few comfortable years at the end when she never had to worry about how she was going to live.'

There was a brief silence and then Kirk said crisply,

'So, having made it up the financial ladder I'd like a wife with a perfect background, a rose in my buttonhole, if you like.'

His hardness didn't mesh with the compassion she'd glimpsed with his treatment of his aunt. She respected a certain ruthlessness in business. She respected still more his capacity for caring.

'I don't expect an answer immediately,' he said.

There was a moment's silence and then Imogen said abruptly, meeting the directness of his dark eyes, 'I'll marry you.'

Her voice was a little tense but very decided. She couldn't analyse the reasons for her answer, but she knew she didn't want to retract.

'Good,' he said with a brief smile.

He hadn't crossed the room to draw her into his arms and kiss her. He hadn't said he loved her. The terms of their marriage from the outset were very clear.

Against her will she thought back to their first months together when, despite everything that was against it, their marriage seemed to have a rich potential. In the early weeks following Graeme's death, she had only been going through the mechanics of living. Marriage to Kirk changed that. He advised her on business matters. He taught her things she hadn't known about herself. He made her laugh again. Her father had always undermined her confidence; Kirk built it up.

She had never lived with a man before, though even if she had it wouldn't have prepared her for her life with Kirk. She learned that he could be protective, tender, making her feel utterly safe as he held her in his arms, or that he could pull her close with a sudden need of her, making her discover unknown elements in herself as, with each time they made love, he seemed to draw her to a greater response.

There had only been one flaw in their marriage, but it had permeated their relationship like an indelible dye. She still loved Graeme, or rather she believed she did. She hadn't known then what love meant.

Kirk had thought that in time she would get over Graeme. He was right. In time she had. But by then there were other strains on their relationship and, in the atmosphere of tension between them, there had never been a quiet moment of trust when she could have admitted to him that her feelings for Graeme hadn't been as intense as she'd supposed. Somehow it wasn't possible with so much discord between them for her to show him how much their marriage meant to her.

The business, after such a promising start, was doing badly. She refused to concede that Jim was a drain on it. She remembered their last argument on the topic. She had got home late. Kirk glanced pointedly at his watch as she joined him in the lounge. Kicking her shoes off, she sat down on the sofa.

'This is the third evening this week you've not been home till nine. Doesn't Jim share any of the work with you at all?' he asked curtly.

'OK, so I'm late. So what?' she said unreasonably, uneasiness about the company finances making her quick to retaliate.

'The "so what" is that New Radiance doesn't seem to leave any room in your life for anything else.'

'Don't dress it up. You're getting at Jim again.'

'For God's sake!' Kirk began in impatient annoyance. 'Not this again.'

'Well, who brought the subject up?' she demanded, getting to her feet as she confronted him. 'You want me to give Jim the push. You think he's dead weight.'

'And evidently I'm not the only one,' he said with the light sarcasm he so often used these days to mask his annoyance with her.

'And what's that supposed to mean?'

'Why do you think he was sacked from his last job?' Kirk asked brutally.

'That's damned unfair!' Imogen exclaimed hotly, her eyes blazing. 'Jim was made redundant and you know it.'

'Don't be so naïve. He was sacked.'

She stared at him in stormy silence and then turned to go out of the room. Kirk stopped her.

'Look,' he began quietly, taking hold of her arm, 'it's been a long day and we're both tired.' He pulled her nearer and bent to her throat, his voice dropping to a warmer pitch. 'Let's forget about work and get an early night.'

She pushed him away and said coldly,

'If you want an early night you go ahead, but I'm not coming to bed now.'

It was the first time they'd had an argument that hadn't been rectified later by making love. Her coldness made the situation worse. Soon Kirk no longer demanded physical closeness from her and she wasn't certain enough of herself, despite her loneliness for him, to make the first move to rekindle the intimate side of their marriage.

Kirk started to work late and, preoccupied with the business, Imogen didn't immediately doubt his convenient excuse. Intuition told her there was a latent attraction between him and one of the newly employed and highly competent accountants who was now working with him. Lydia drove another wedge between them, but Imogen hadn't acknowledged that their marriage was over. That came later when she was sent the receipt for a double hotel room in the name of Mr and Mrs Cameron.

She opened the innocuous-looking envelope over breakfast, glancing briefly at the receipt before reading Lydia's malicious letter.

'What is it?' Kirk asked quietly, concern in his voice as he studied her face. 'Not bad news?'

'Not bad news!' she said in a voice cramped with emotion, as she pushed her chair back and slapped the letter down in front of him. 'Oh, that's rich! You take your damned mistress with you on a so-called business trip. Well, here's your receipt.'

'What?' he said, snatching it up, his face darkening with anger.

'So I'm not woman enough to satisfy you, am I?' she said, fighting furiously to suppress tears of bitter hurt and betrayal. 'She's got a nice turn of phrase, your mistress.'

Kirk got swiftly to his feet and grabbed hold of her wrist.

'Now, you listen to me.'

'No!'

Imogen snatched herself free and continued fiercely in a torment of anger and heartbreak.

'I may not have loved you when I married you, but I had every intention of being faithful to you. You couldn't even be that!'

He looked at her for a long, cold instant.

'When you've calmed down, we'll talk this through.'

But they hadn't talked. Instead of that, she'd walked out on him.

Kirk pulled on to the deep frontage outside the salon.

'You're really determined to go ahead with this divorce?' he queried curtly.

'We couldn't expect our marriage to work,' said Imogen, her voice neutral.

He studied her a moment with hard, narrowed eyes. Once again she was conscious of the dangerous tension between them, of his superior strength and the forcefulness of his personality. She lifted her chin a little as she met his gaze. Loving him had only brought her unhappiness. Now she was protected from his ever hurting her again because, if his tenderness and strength had once taught her to love him, from his indifference she had learned to hate him.

'I'll call you later in the week,' he said, before adding with faint contempt, 'Don't worry, I know you're anxious to start divorce proceedings. I'll let you know how I feel about it just as soon as I've thought things through.'

She nodded and got out of the car, turning to say a cool goodbye as she shut the door. The words had never sounded so final to her.

CHAPTER THREE

IMOGEN walked into the shop. Jackie, one of her top stylists, immediately came over to her.

'Trouble, I'm afraid,' she began. 'Mrs Milbank's complained that Tracey's used the wax too hot and that her legs are marked.'

After her meeting with Kirk, Imogen scarcely felt she could summon the necessary restraint for a show of sympathetic tactfulness with a difficult customer. But all she needed right now was a claim against the company.

'OK, Jackie,' she said, 'I'll handle it.'

'How was lunch?' Jackie asked meaningfully.

'Taxing,' she admitted with wry understatement.

Briskly she walked through to the beauty salon, trying to dismiss Kirk from her mind. She greeted Mrs Milbank with pleasant, professional courtesy. There had been nothing wrong with the wax treatment she had been given apart from the fact that she felt she merited the attention of the senior beautician. Half an hour later, with an appointment made for a complimentary facial, she left the shop.

Imogen went into her office. Taking out the bank statements she started going through them again, but somehow she couldn't focus her mind on the figures. She was thinking of Kirk. Thoughtfully, she touched her lips with tentative fingers, as though she could still recall the hardness of his mouth on hers. With a gesture of impatience she pushed the papers aside.

The door opening brought her back to the immediate and she glanced up to see Jim, who came jauntily into the office. In his mid-thirties, he was a tall man with a strong, vigorous build. He had a broad, good-tempered face with blue eyes that looked arrestingly clear against his tan. His clothes were expensive and gave the impression that neither earning nor spending money was a problem to him.

'Thought I'd look in and see you,' he began cheerfully as he perched opposite her on the desk. 'I've brought you the projected cash-flow forecast I've been working on.'

'I don't know how you can take all this so lightly,' she said, accepting the document he held out to her. 'Do you realise just how near the company is to going under?'

'We've got a bit of a cash-flow problem,' Jim said easily, 'that's all. These are tough times. Everyone's living on credit.'

'No,' Imogen corrected him, 'it's got nothing to do with the economic climate. You're taking too much money out of the company, Jim. You're using it to finance too high a lifestyle, and it's got to stop. We can't keep borrowing our way out of trouble.'

'Nonsense,' Jim said confidently. 'The company's still growing, so we can service the debt.' He leaned across the desk and patted her arm. 'Listen, you're a great manager and you do a first-class job running the three salons, but you don't understand finance. I know what I'm doing. Trust me.'

Imogen looked up at him with troubled eyes. His buoyant assurance was convincing. It was tempting to believe him, especially when she wanted to. But the bank statements didn't support his confidence.

'I've got a fair amount invested in the company, too, remember?' he continued. 'I'm not going to see it fold.'

'Well, that's what it's going to do,' Immogen said flatly, before indicating the document, and adding,

'I'll look through the figures and then we're going to have to come to a better agreement about controlling the company finances.'

Jim studied her a moment.

'You were seeing Kirk today, weren't you?' he queried.

'I had lunch with him,' Imogen said. 'And no, Kirk isn't the reason why I'm questioning the company's performance.'

Jim didn't disagree with her. Instead he said,

'How do you feel about dinner tonight? Cheer you up.'

Imogen gave a reluctant smile.

'At the moment, it would take more than that,' she commented, before saying, 'No, I'm working late tonight, but thanks for the offer, anyway.'

'OK then,' he said. 'See you Thursday.'

He went out of the office. Involuntarily, she remembered Kirk's advice to her, given over a year ago. 'Buy him out. He's a liability. You'd do better on your own.' It was the opinion of a man with a shrewd business sense and a flair for making money.

Yet without Jim, she doubted that she would ever have got the venture off the ground. But it wasn't just that. Jim was her brother, the only close relation she had, apart from her father. She had been five when her mother had died, too young to have any clear memories of her. For some reason, she and her father had never got along. No matter how hard she tried to win his approval, she always failed.

Jim clowned his way through school, refused to take anything seriously, and though their father was disappointed in him, it didn't alter his affection for him. Imogen's academic successes somehow never counted. The only reason she had wanted to do well was to please him, to earn his love, as though she knew she didn't have it spontaneously as her brother did. It would have been easy, given the set-up and the noticeably preferential treatment Jim always had, for them not to have got on. But they did. Jim, with his easy-going nature and genuine affability, listened to her, whereas her father ignored her; Jim encouraged, whereas he criticised.

Shortly after New Radiance was set up, the company Jim had been working for had been taken over. It had seemed natural for him to come into the business with her full-time. It was unthinkable that she could regard him as a liability, whatever Kirk said.

The phone rang and she picked it up, expecting it to be a business call. Instead, it was Peter.

'Hi,' he began. 'I've been thinking of you. How did you get on?'

Unconsciously she smiled at the sound of his warm, flexible voice.

'I've told Kirk I want a divorce. He says he'll think it over.'

'He must know you're never going to get back together again,' Peter said, a shade intrusively, considering he was only a friend.

Imogen had met him six months back when she'd enrolled on an evening class to learn Greek. Since breaking up with Kirk, she had avoided any situation that might bring with it the risk of a date and involvement in a new relationship. Being on the course together had given her and Peter an interest in common. She liked his company and when, in the final term, he'd casually asked her out for a drink after class, she'd accepted. But now he was trespassing on her feelings when he had no right to.

'Kirk and I did have two years together,' she said. 'You can't just wipe that out.'

'You sound as if you regret that it's all over. You ought to have worked out where you stand by now.'

'I have worked out where I stand. Look, it's my

problem. I'll solve it in my own time.'

'You're still tied to him, aren't you?' Peter said. 'He means you can't get a relationship going with anyone.'

There was a tap at the door and Jackie came in.

'The Belissima rep's here to see you,' she said quietly.

Imogen put a hand over the mouthpiece.

'I'll be with him in just a minute,' she told Jackie. She turned her attention back to the phone call.

'Have I called at a difficult time?' Peter asked.

'Afraid so. Can I call you back?'

'Sure,' he agreed.

'OK,' said Imogen. 'Speak to you later.'

Hearing from him seemed to have made her feel more, not less hemmed in by problems. She could do without being pressurised by Peter. At the moment she was divided between feeling that she never wanted to become seriously involved with a man again, and then wishing she could commit herself wholeheartedly to another relationship, if only to demonstrate that she didn't need Kirk in her life any more. Her conflicting emotions were evidence that she wasn't ready for any special involvement with Peter.

Thinking about Peter stopped her for a short interval from replaying in memory her marriage to Kirk. She wondered what was the soonest she could expect to hear from him. She supposed it was the uncertainty that meant she couldn't push the memories of their marriage from her mind. Once she was divorced, Kirk would be consigned quite definitely to the past and she could get on with her life again. As the week went by, every time the phone rang she picked it up anticipating that it would be him.

Peter had got tickets for a West End musical for Friday evening. Imogen got in from work and walked straight through into her bedroom to start getting changed. She hadn't got away from the salon till after six and to be meeting him at the theatre at eight was cutting things a bit fine.

She had moved into her flat a couple of months ago. Once she had decided she wasn't going back to Kirk it had seemed sensible to start buying a place of her own. It was a symbol of her independence.

In the past year she'd had no contact at all with Kirk. They'd had one final, stormy meeting after she'd walked out on him, when Kirk had told her she could have a separation. He had said he'd give her a year to sort out her feelings and he had kept to it. She had tried to be glad but if she was honest, those first months without him had been a wasteland of loneliness that not even the demands and problems of work could lessen. Even now, when she was determined to put him out of her life completely, pain twisted her heart when she thought of what they had once shared.

She showered quickly before slipping on a shapely dress with a fluted skirt. She outlined her eyes in smoky colour and was fastening her ear-rings when the door bell rang. Without stopping to step into her court shoes, she went to answer it.

She opened the door and then stiffened a little as she saw Kirk there. His gaze took her in with a sweeping glance, reminding her that whatever barriers of coolness lay between them, he was a man and he found her attractive. She wished she had stopped to put her shoes on. He was so very much taller than she was and, barefoot, she felt at a disadvantage with him.

'May I come in?' he asked a shade pointedly.

'I suppose so,' she said ungraciously, stepping back.

She preceded him into the lounge, and in an attempt to appear more at ease asked,

'Would you like a drink?'

'Scotch, if you've got it.'

She didn't have to ask him how he wanted it; she'd

lived with him long enough to know his tastes. It was curious to think she knew him more intimately than any man she had ever known, curious and ironic, and unreasonably she resented him for it.

She poured herself a small Martini to look companionable and handed him his glass before sitting down opposite him. After the initial shock of seeing him, her self-possession was returning.

'Have you thought any more about what I asked you?' she began, deliberately taking the initiative.

'Yes. I want you to come back to me.'

It wasn't a request. It was a statement from a man used to making demands and having them met without raising his voice.

For an instant Imogen stared at him in complete disbelief. Then she set her glass down abruptly.

'Is this a joke?' she asked, her voice rising sharply.

'I don't make jokes about things like this,' he said, his voice harsh with a repressed savagery.

'Well, you can forget it,' Imogen told him, getting swiftly to her feet. 'I'd be crazy to come back to you. I've played the part of the perfect wife and the perfect hostess for quite long enough. That's all you ever wanted me for, and I'm through with it!'

'Not yet you're not,' said Kirk, his eyes as he looked at her as hard as his voice. 'There's the possibility of another contract with Transit International for consultancy work. It's worth a great deal of money. The Managing Director was very taken with you when you met him at the convention in Paris eighteen months ago. I'm entertaining him and his wife in a couple of months' time, and your being there and putting on the façade of the perfect hostess, as you call it, could be enough to make the difference between my getting the contract or not. You've had as much freedom as I'm prepared to give you.'

'You really think I'm going to come back to you to

help you win a business contract?' she said with contemptuous disbelief.

He stood up and crossed the room to her, taking hold of her insistently by the shoulders, making her confront him whether she wanted to or not.

'If I lose this contract,' he said, his voice low and warning, 'I will make this divorce you're so anxious to obtain as difficult and expensive as I know how. Financially, you're in trouble, anyway. Push me on this and I'll break you. I married you to be an asset, not a liability.'

Imogen snatched herself free.

'Why don't you get Lydia to stand in for me?'

'Because she's not my wife. You are, and Bob Elland's got very definite views about marriage and divorce.'

'Damn Bob Elland and his contract! I'm not being used!'

He countered her remark by saying with swift violence,

Now you listen to me. As far as Bob Elland is concerned, divorce is anathema. You've met him. His involvement in the church and the way he takes his religion isn't news to you. It's not an extra where he's concerned. It governs his life, and that extends into business dealings. I'm not losing a contract through offending his religious principles.'

'Then tell him I'm on holiday,' she said with reckless sarcasm, 'an indefinite one.'

'You knew what I expected from you when I married you,' he said angrily. 'I'm not prepared to lose a contract because you're tired of playing the role of my wife. And I'm certainly not losing you to another man. If I'd known you were seeing someone else, I'd have put a stop to this sooner.'

She wasn't thinking anything like clearly enough for it to occur to her that there was any discrepancy between his last remark and what he'd said before. She was another of his acquisitions, and her resentment of his proprietorial attitude went all the deeper because she had once loved him.

'Find someone else to play the part,' she retorted sharply. 'You've influenced my life and moulded me to your wishes long enough. I'm tired of being your property!'

'Yes, I did change you,' Kirk conceded angrily, his fingers biting into her shoulders. 'I made you into a woman. That was more than your precious dead fiancé achieved. Or can't you handle a real relationship with a man? Was part of his appeal the fact that he never made any physical demands on you?'

'I don't have to discuss this with you——' she began.

He interrupted her.

'Then answer me this—if you were so totally in love with him, why were you still a virgin when I married you?'

She couldn't find an answer. He was too close to learning the truth, but she wouldn't allow him the victory of knowing that in the time they had been together she had come to love him. Breaking his hold on her, though she knew he could have held her pinioned still had he wanted to, she said with angry emphasis, 'I'm not coming back to you. I want to be free.'

'Free?' he questioned quickly. 'I thought the reason you were asking for a divorce was so you could marry again.'

'I've had enough of marriage to last me a lifetime,' she assured him.

She saw his jaw tighten at her complete indictment of their relationship.

'Tell me,' he said savagely, as he caught hold of her roughly, 'do you respond to Peter the way you used to respond to me? I started the fire. I'd like to know if he's getting warm by it.'

'Let go of me!' she snapped, furious to find that her voice was unsteady.

Her heart was beating like a hammer. She struggled ineffectually to pull away, fear of her own vulnerability when confronted with the impact of his masculinity making her desperate to wrench herself free. She had proved to him once that the embered physical attraction between them wasn't dead. She wasn't succumbing to his touch again.

Kirk crushed her into his arms, forcibly moulding her to him, and then, before she could turn her head away, his lips came down on hers, kissing her relentlessly, as though he intended demanding complete possession of her. Her heart was clamouring so wildly that she could offer no more than token resistance. The pressure of his close, pressing hands, his hard, demanding lips, told her that physically he wanted her as much as he had in those first months of their marriage.

In the year they had been apart she had half-forgotten this aching longing for completeness, this dangerous pleasure in his touch. Her capitulation was sudden, the initial tug of dismay at her surrender forced from her mind by the hardness of his lips against her throat, his hand that slipped sensuously from her shoulder to the softness of her breast.

At the back of her consciousness was the knowledge that she must let this go no further.

'Imogen.' Kirk's voice was a racked, harsh whisper.

There was no element of compulsion now about being held closely in his arms. Her pliant body was pressed to his. She could feel his driving need of her and her lips answered his in a crazy torrent of desire as he kissed her again, exploding the fragile restraint between them.

She wanted him, but physical union with him wasn't going to wipe out everything that had gone before. There was still no love in their relationship. There was still Lydia, their constant disagreements over New Radiance. There was still the fact that he viewed her solely in terms of her usefulness to him. She would only despise herself if she let Kirk take her now, for they could have no lasting future together.

Shakily she pushed against him, her strength returning as her senses cleared, bringing back reality.

'I won't let this happen,' she said, her voice a husky whisper, her eyes stormy and intense. 'I don't need you in my life. I don't belong with you. I never did.'

'It didn't seem like that a moment ago,' he said, his voice savage and intense.

He took a step nearer, so that his strength and dominating height seemed more menacing. They were alone in her flat, he was her husband and the tension between them had already made the summer evening treacherous with possibilities. In sudden desperation she said, as he caught hold of her by the shoulders,

'You're right—you *did* teach me how to respond to a man. Maybe that's why Peter and I are so good in bed together.'

She saw his eyes darken and his mouth harden with an emotion that was more complicated than anger. His fingers tightened on her shoulders so that under any other circumstances she would have protested at their bruising force. For an instant he held her rigid, and then he shook her till her hair tumbled across her forehead and into her eyes. She cried out incoherently and he released her abruptly, his face taut and drained as if equally harrowed by his rough treatment of her as by what she had just told him.

She stumbled into a chair, saying unsteadily in a voice that rose within a notch of breaking,

'Get out. I never want to see you again.'

He knelt down beside her, smoothing her hair back from her face, his eyes searching hers. She flinched at his touch.

'Get out!' she repeated fiercely.

He didn't answer immediately. She met the probe of his unyielding gaze with mute hostility, and then he said with grim finality, his voice low, though she could feel the curbed force behind it.

'I don't care who you've slept with, I'm not letting you go.'

Imogen watched as he got to his feet and walked out of the room with the quick, purposeful step of a man used to taking control. There was the sound of the front door closing and after that, silence. Imogen closed her eyes for an instant, as though she could hide from what had just happened. Kirk's glass was beside her untouched Martini on the coffee table. She picked it up and swallowed some of the whisky. Its warming fire lapped through her slowly, steadying her. It was some time before she remembered Peter.

She arrived at the theatre late. Peter was standing in the empty foyer. He was of average height with a trim build that held none of the latent strengths of Kirk's six foot two, hard litheness. He had brown eyes, a quick smile and a manner that suggested both nerviness and energy. His hair was thick and a shade unruly, almost fair in colour, but Imogen had never felt the slightest impulse to run her fingers through it as she did with Kirk's.

'What happened to you?' Peter began. 'You were supposed to meet me nearly forty-five minutes ago.'

'I know. I'm sorry, I got held up.'

'Well, you might have phoned.'

'I did. I called your office, but there was no reply.'

She hadn't told him the reason why she was late

and she didn't intend to. Somehow, she couldn't.
What had happened was between her and Kirk. She
coloured a little as she remembered the lie she had
told Kirk, that she and Peter were sleeping together.
To attempt an edited version would only prompt a
barrage of questions.

Tucking her hand through his arm, she said,

'I'm sorry, really I am. Let's take our seats before
we miss any more of the show.'

'We've missed enough as it is,' Peter remarked
crossly. 'Do you realise what I had to pay for these
tickets?'

She repressed a quick-tempered comment. The inci-
dent with Kirk had made her on edge, not least
because his determination to force her back to him
was so unassailable. But she wasn't going to allow
him to cause a row with Peter.

They went into the darkened auditorium and edged
along the middle row of the dress circle to their seats.
In the dimness, Imogen flickered a glance at Peter and
saw his face relax into a smile as he looked stagewards.
With an effort, she tried to force her attention to the
play.

What was she doing here, feigning enjoyment in a
musical comedy when her thoughts were in such
chaos? She refused to admit she was still in love with
Kirk. A familiar aching sadness tugged at her heart
as she thought of her wrecked marriage, of the emptiness in her life no other man could fill.

She didn't want to remember how nearly she had
given in to him this evening. Was she really as over
him as she had supposed? At the back of her mind
wasn't there the unacknowledged wish to be back with
him again, even if he was still involved with Lydia?
She denied the notion. She was never going back to
him.

He'd married her in much the same way as he

acquired equities on the stock exchange. She'd hit a
low and he'd moved in. But she wasn't emotionally
devastated any more. She had recovered from
Graeme's death. She'd even learned to come to terms
with the fact that Kirk felt nothing for her. For a
short while she was confident enough of her own inner
strength to believe her hard-won independence from
him was impossible to violate, despite his threats.

The exuberant finale was followed by noisy applause
as the curtain swept down and, with a slight start,
Imogen joined in the clapping.

'First-class entertainment,' Peter remarked.

'Very good,' she agreed, weighting her statement
with a little more conviction by adding, 'The numbers
were very catchy.'

They followed the press of people heading up the
aisle towards the exit. Peter took hold of her hand,
and she didn't withdraw it, though the gesture wasn't
without a touch of defiance aimed at Kirk. She was
independent. She wasn't going back to him, and if she
intended entering into a closer relationship with Peter,
he couldn't stop her.

As they stepped out of the theatre, Peter said,

'I'm afraid we've got a bit of a walk to the car.'

'It's a nice night,' she said, determined to forget
Kirk and what had happened that evening. 'I'll enjoy
a walk.'

'We ought to do something like this to celebrate
that it's almost six months since we first met,' said
Peter. 'Maybe follow it with dinner somewhere.'

'No, I've got a better idea. I'll cook dinner and then
we'll go on to the theatre. Do you realise I haven't
cooked you a meal since I've known you?'

'Yes, you have,' he contradicted, smiling at her.
'Don't you remember, shortly after I met you at that
evening class, that time you had trouble with your car
and I drove you home?'

'I only put a pizza under the grill. That doesn't count.'

'Well, it tasted pretty good to me,' Peter said. 'Or perhaps it was the company.'

They strolled along the wide street with its brightly illuminated shop windows and constant traffic.

'What are you doing tomorrow?' he asked.

'I'll be working late.'

Her defiance against Kirk wasn't working. Peter was only a friend. It was good to see him for a drink or for dinner, but she wasn't ready to put their relationship on a closer footing. If she did, she'd only be using him as an emotional bulwark against Kirk.

'You won't be working all evening,' Peter pointed out.

'I know, but when I finish I want to go through the books with Jim. Let's leave seeing each other till next week.'

'OK,' he agreed a shade brusquely, before asking after a slight pause, 'Have you heard from your husband yet?'

'He doesn't want a divorce,' Imogen said, evading the question.

'You're going to have to take a much tougher line with him.'

Imogen laughed shortly.

'You don't take a tough line with Kirk,' she told him. 'Nobody does. But anyway, I don't feel like talking about him. Right now, what I'd like best is to be able to forget him completely.'

'Suits me,' he said.

It was late by the time they pulled up outside her flat. They chatted for a while in the car.

'Aren't you going to ask me in for coffee?' Peter prompted.

'I might,' she said, her eyes teasing.

They laughed, and Imogen said amiably,

'Of course. In any case, I've got that tape you lent me to give back.'

Talking about music, they walked up the stairs to her flat. Imogen preceded him into the lounge. The placid stillness of the room that bore no trace of her scene with Kirk impressed itself on her. It seemed hard to believe that they had come so close to making love or that he had shaken her so savagely. The room recorded nothing. It was the way he persisted in her thoughts that made the room's tranquillity seem strange.

Going over to the hi-fi, she slipped a record out of its sleeve and said with a smile,

'I feel like listening to something cheerful. Do you like Incantation's "Music of the Andes"?'

'That's fine by me,' he commented, as she put the record on the turntable.

He strolled over to the sofa where a book lay on the cushions, and picked it up to glance at the title.

'You're reading Fitzgerald,' he remarked interestedly as she went through into the kitchen to make the coffee, leaving the door ajar. 'Did you see *The Great Gatsby* when it was on?' he asked as he joined her.

His voice became a shade preoccupied. Imogen saw his eyes go to the two glasses left from Kirk's visit. It was too late now to wish she had rinsed them and put them away.

Peter glanced at her and said curtly,

'That's why you were late, wasn't it? Your husband called round.'

'I didn't know he was looking in,' she said, determinedly keeping her voice casual. 'It held me up.'

'It must have been quite a friendly little session,' he remarked unpleasantly, 'if you offered him a drink.'

'Peter, I can do without this. I've had a rough day and I don't need your comments to add to it.'

He held up a placating hand and said,

'All right, I'll keep quiet, but I think it's about time you made it clear to your husband where you stand. I know being divorced isn't easy. I've been there, remember, but dragging things out doesn't make it any better.'

'I realise you're trying to help,' Imogen said, 'but please, let's drop this. And just for the record, no, it wasn't a friendly little session. It was anything but.'

There was a short pause and then Peter said tersely, 'OK, I'll take your word for it.'

He walked over to the doorway and studied her a moment before saying,

'Look, don't bother with the coffee. It's late and I ought to be going.'

'It's almost made.'

'I know, but I think it would be better if I went.'

He paused as though expecting her to contradict him. She didn't, and he said, his tone a shade clipped, 'I'll call you in the week.'

Imogen nodded wearily. She felt a renewed surge of hostility towards Kirk. This was his fault. She had wanted to prove to herself she was capable of making a relationship with another man work, and he was forcing her to acknowledge that she couldn't. He was still the dominant influence in her life.

She saw Peter out and then went back into the lounge and mechanically turned off the stereo. It had not been a good evening either for herself or for Peter. Her resentment against Kirk reasserted itself more strongly.

It was disheartening that, when it came to her dealings with him, she was so easily thrown off balance. She had intended distancing herself from their past together so they could talk things through calmly, coldly, and with as little emotion as possible. She had failed twice and the knowledge dismayed her and acted as a goad to make her determined not to do so again. She wasn't capitulating to him. He wasn't the only one who could set terms.

Impulsively she picked up the phone, before hesitating and replacing the receiver. It was too late to ring him now and insist that they talk, that he face up to the reality that their relationship was over. And maybe a phone call wasn't the best way of contacting him again, however reassuring it was to have a sizeable distance between them. She'd drive into London the next morning to see him at his head office.

She made a quick mental check of her schedule. There was nothing she couldn't shelve, and anyway, getting a divorce from Kirk had to come first.

CHAPTER FOUR

THE LIFT took Imogen up from the underground car park to the spaciousness of the reception area. Kirk's management consultancy firm handled some very lucrative contracts, and the décor reflected the corporate image of competence and success. Already, Imogen was conscious of her heartbeat quickening with the prospect of confronting Kirk.

She was crossing over to the reception desk when a woman pushed through the swing-doors from one of the suites of offices. With a jolt of dismay, Imogen recognised Lydia Slater. She was wearing an expensively casual suit with a silk shirt-blouse and a man's tie that cleverly heightened her femininity. In her early thirties, she had all the assurance of a woman accustomed to success in a man's world. Her hair, a lovely shade of brown, was cut into a flattering wind-blown style. She had smooth, ivory skin and dark, intelligent eyes that were enhanced by dramatic glasses. She looked efficient, capable and sultry.

She saw Imogen, halted an instant, and then came purposefully towards her.

'Well, surprise, surprise,' she began nastily. 'It must be over a year since I last saw you.'

'A shame it hasn't been longer,' Imogen said, meeting Lydia's hostile gaze squarely.

Lydia slid her hands into her skirt pockets and considered Imogen with a pretence of detachment.

'My, you get the claws out quickly these days,' she commented. 'I didn't think you were that sort. What happened to the girlish charm?'

'It disappeared when you started sleeping with my husband.'

'Don't blame me because you couldn't keep Kirk happy. He's a stimulating, dynamic man, dedicated to high standards. He needs a partner to complement him, not just intellectually, but . . . ' she paused deliberately before adding with malicious triumph, 'in bed as well. From what I gather, you didn't rate too highly on either score.'

'I'm not interested in your analysis of my marriage,' Imogen said, her voice low and completely controlled, despite the sudden colour that had come into her face. 'I came here to see Kirk. I've got nothing to say to you.'

'Then don't hang around, because Kirk's not in this morning,' Lydia said bluntly, before adding with a recovery of her polished manner, 'though I'll give him a message if you like.'

'There is no message,' said Imogen, her words clear and evenly spaced.

She turned and walked briskly to the lift, her eyes full of anger and distress. So Lydia was still as much a part of Kirk's life as she'd ever been! She had to get out of the building. Once she was at work she wouldn't be able to think of Kirk and Lydia together.

The lift came and she got in. She opened her clutch-bag and found her car keys. They were in her hand as she ran towards her car, her steps echoing hollowly on the concrete. She didn't immediately see Kirk locking the door of his parked Mercedes.

'Imogen?'

She ignored him, quickening her pace. Her car was just ahead, but he caught up with her before she could reach it. Taking hold of her arm, he swung her round to face him.

'What's the hurry?' he began. 'And what are *you* doing here?'

'Why don't you ask your mistress?' She flung the words at him.

Annoyance hardened the stern lines of his face. The oppressively low roof and the shadowy lines of parked cars in the chilly basement made the tension between them still more menacing. She felt the strength of his grip as she tried to draw away from him.

'I'm asking you,' he said harshly. 'It's time we talked. You're in no fit state to drive.'

'We've nothing to talk about,' she said, her voice unsteady in its vehemence. 'I came to say I'm going ahead with the divorce. I don't care if you contest it, or what it costs me. There couldn't be any price too high for getting you out of my life!'

'Don't give me that!' he cut across her furiously. 'You were ready for me to take you last night. And maybe I should have.'

'Then you lost the opportunity.'

'But not this one.'

She gave a startled gasp as he pulled her into his arms, giving her no time to put a fiercely protesting hand against his chest. She could feel his hard body throughout every inch of her as his lips came down on her, kissing her closely and angrily. A helpless vertigo hit her as her senses recorded his dominating, engulfing strength and the feel of his firm, relentless lips on hers. A treacherous melting pleasure was flickering throughout her whole body. Unthinkingly, she slid her hands up around his neck as his lips parted hers. Almost instantly he seemed to answer her change in response, and his mouth became gentler but just as arousing.

And then Lydia flashed into her confused mind. With desperate strength she pulled away from him. She realised he still only had to touch her for part of her to want him, and in her fury to deny it, she snatched herself completely free.

'Don't you ever come near me or contact me again,' she said, her voice wildly unsteady. 'You'll be hearing from my solicitor.'

She ran the last steps to her car, unlocking the door with fingers that trembled.

'Imogen! Wait!'

She started the car with an angry roar of acceleration, tightening her grip on the wheel as she drove up the ramp at some speed and pulled on to the street.

She forced her attention to the busy London traffic. Only as she stopped at the second set of lights did she touch her lips tentatively as though she still felt the sensual pressure of Kirk's kiss. She turned the radio on and headed along the arterial road out of London.

The traffic was less heavy at this time of day. Soon she was off the dual carriageway and driving along the familiar suburban roads to the main salon. A short distance ahead of her was a blue Saab. An intermittent stream of traffic passed her in the opposite direction.

The sudden switch from routine to nightmare happened so instantaneously that her actions seemed reflex. Ahead of her, on the other side of the road, she saw a cyclist shoot out of a turning. The oncoming lorry swerved violently to avoid the bike. Imogen slammed on the brakes and pulled the wheel hard over, comprehending even as she did so that she was going to be hit.

She had a brief impression of the lorry racing towards her at close range, its cab colossal through her narrow windscreen, a paralysing certainty of death that seemed to choke a muffled cry from her. And then there was the terror-striking crash when the whole cab seemed to be ploughing in on her. She heard the deafening crunch of compressed metal, just moments before being struck a blinding blow to her head as she was thrown forward. The iron restraint of the seat-belt was crushing the breath out of her. Sickening radials of pain echoed through her, as an engulfing void sent her falling into darkness with a roaring in her ears.

Short gaps of consciousness brought her back to dazed glimpses of reality. She was shivering with cold, and the pavement struck with the chill of a mortuary slab against her back. Someone was bending over her and above was the bright expanse of sky. There was the sound of voices and, faintly, the wail of a siren, growing stronger by the minute. In a haze of pain and fear she felt the warm wetness of blood glueing her petticoat to her skin.

The wail of the ambulance sounded on and on, part of her being, as much as her feeble heartbeat. She was sinking into a blackness pierced by sharp lights of pain that seemed suddenly to come from above.

She opened her eyes to see the masked face of the anaesthetist. She seemed to be floating, her mind drifting away from her body. The presence of death seemed everywhere. She wanted Kirk, but she was too far under to call his name. Above her she saw the sign 'Operating Theatre Two'.

Afterwards, she couldn't remember being wheeled back to the wards. Vaguely she was aware of muffled sound, of efficient footsteps in the corridor outside. Into her drugged mind came the pressing weight of things unfinished. She wanted Kirk before she slipped beyond regrets or explanations or amends. The frequent blood pressure and pulse checks by the nurse were a faint scratch on the surface of her consciousness. She was unaware that anyone was by her bedside.

It was dark when she opened her eyes again. The lamp on the dressing-table was on and Kirk was sitting beside her, his hand spread out against his forehead as though he was worn out with anxiety and waiting. His face in the shadowy light looked drawn, his cheeks more hollow than they were. It seemed as though he sensed she was watching him, for he glanced up suddenly.

'Kirk——' she began faintly.

He stood up and grasped tightly hold of her hand as he bent over her, and the emotion she saw in his face made a strangled sob come into her throat. The warm vitality of his touch made her fingers close feebly on his in response. Kirk was with her and she had the hazy comprehension that he had been all along. For an instant there was no need for words. He was with her and she needed him, and nothing could obscure that elemental truth.

Then he smiled faintly and released her hand to touch her cheek.

'You don't know how worried I've been about you,' he said, his voice a shade husky from the release of tension and long silence.

His gaze held hers for a long moment. At last she whispered.

'Was the other driver all right?'

Kirk nodded.

'You came off the worst of anyone, but don't try to talk.'

'You'll stay, won't you?' she asked, her eyes meeting his in mute appeal as she felt weariness tugging at her.

'I won't leave you,' he confirmed.

The light threw his shadow, towering and black, on to the wall behind him. The impression of him standing over her stayed with her as sleep washed over her. The release from pain and fear brought with it a profound peace. She knew she didn't have to fight any more. She was going to be all right.

The simplicity of those first days in hospital, when thought was narrowed down to a thankfulness to be

alive and an unquestioning acceptance that Kirk had
been with her when she had needed him so desperately, gave way—as she grew stronger—to the intricacy
of normality. Her convalescence was going to be slow,
for she had sustained both head and internal injuries
in the crash.

The transitory understanding she had felt with Kirk
immediately after the accident had faded. When she
thought back to the evening when she had regained
consciousness after the anaesthetic, her impressions of
Kirk standing over her and taking her hand in his had
the same shadowy unsubstantiality as the rest of her
disjointed recollections following the crash.

She remembered how, just by being there, he had
made her feel she was enfolded in his close protectiveness. It had been almost as though their break-up had
never happened. She put the book she was reading
down on the covers and rested her head against the
pillows. What did Kirk feel for her? Had the anaesthetic distorted her perceptions, or had the emotion she
had read in his face when she had first come round to
find he was with her been real and substantial? She
wasn't sure. It all had too much of a dream-like
quality above it for her to trust it, especially now,
when all the tensions in their relationship had reasserted themselves.

Besides, Kirk had never been short on impersonal
kindness, she thought a shade bitterly. He knew she
and her father didn't get along and that apart from
Jim she had no other family ties. That alone would be
enough to account for his concern for her welfare.
Lydia had his love, and shared true intimacy with him
of mind and body. Imogen had the impartial benevo-
lence he might show to a former employee.

The door of her room opened gently and Jim came
in.

'Thought I'd better come in quietly in case you were

asleep,' he began cheerfully. 'How are you feeling?'

'Lonely,' Imogen admitted smilingly, 'so it's good to see you.'

Jim sat down on the bed and studied her with slightly anxious eyes as though, despite her vivacity, he was still concerned about how she was recovering.

'I bought you these,' he said, putting a box of chocolates on the covers in front of her.

'That's very nice of you,' she said appreciatively.

'You've certainly got enough cards,' he commented as he strolled over to the dressing-table to look at a couple at random. 'If you get any more there'll be nowhere to put them.'

'A lot of the customers have sent me them. Kind of them, isn't it? And the flowers are lovely.'

She didn't comment on the fact that her father hadn't even sent her a card. The hurt of his not visiting her was somehow magnified by the flowers and good wishes from customers.

Jim came and sat down by the bedside.

'How are things at the salons?' she asked.

'Fine,' he assured her. 'Jackie's taking care of everything at the main salon. I'm looking in a couple of times in the week and keeping an eye on the other two shops as well, so all you have to do is concentrate on getting well.'

'What did Mr Hollis say about extending our overdraft facilities? Your appointment at the bank was this morning, wasn't it?'

'It's no go,' Jim told her. 'We're at the top of our credit limit, but we may be able to raise the money we need through one of the finance houses.'

'And you know what that's going to cost!' Imogen exclaimed.

'Yes, it'll be expensive,' he agreed patiently, 'but as long as we can meet the interest repayments, we're

OK. Now stop worrying, will you? Just leave everything to me.'

'I'm not agreeing to a loan from a finance house,' she said emphatically, putting a hand up to her forehead which was starting to throb dully. 'I don't want you to do anything until I've seen Mr Hollis myself. Perhaps he'll accept a personal guarantee for security.'

'We need the money now. You're not going to be fit enough to be arranging company loans for at least a month.'

'I'll be out of hospital a lot sooner than that,' she said in a tight voice, tensing against the headache that intensified as she spoke.

'Look, I won't do anything without consulting you first,' Jim agreed placatingly. 'All right?'

Imogen nodded. She couldn't summon up the energy to insist further that he wasn't to act on his own when it came to raising a loan. The headache was ripping her resolve to shreds. She could only lie still, braced against the pain, waiting for it to abate.

There was a tap at the door and one of the neatly uniformed nurses came in.

'Time for your tablets, Mrs Cameron,' she said, as she poured out a glass of water and handed it to Imogen.

Jim stayed a short while longer and then, noting how tense and pale Imogen looked, got up to go.

'Did you bring the solicitor's letter you said we'd had, pressing us for payment?' she asked.

'I've said *I'll* deal with it,' he told her gently. 'Now listen, just relax.

'But did you bring it?'

There was a short pause, and then he said unwillingly,

'Yes, I've got it here, but I don't want you worrying about the business when you're supposed to be trying to get well.'

She reached out and touched his hand.

'I know,' she said, managing a faint smile, 'but I feel helpless enough as it is without being kept in the dark.'

Jim looked at her, concern in his eyes.

'All right,' he said, taking an envelope out of his inside jacket pocket and handing it to her, 'but don't take a lot of legal jargon too seriously. We'll get a payment to our creditors—enough to keep them happy. All it involves is some juggling with what we've got on the company's current account.'

Imogen waited till he had gone before starting to read the letter. Alarm made her skim the words as the first paragraph warned her how seriously the company was in trouble. Despite Jim's assurances the truth was plain enough. New Radiance was falling apart.

She had to get out of hospital and back to work. If the doctor wouldn't agree, she'd discharge herself. But behind her determination, a practical cautiousness insisted she be realistic. It would be weeks before she could take a really active part again in the running of the business.

Her father had always said she didn't have the acumen to run a company. When she'd asked him to attend a hairdressing gala, sponsored by one of the hair-care product manufacturers, and New Radiance had been prominently represented among the award winners, he'd seemed to revise his opinion. His terse congratulations had meant more to her than all the subsequent features in the trade magazines and local papers. She had to keep the business from folding. He'd already condemned her for the failure of her marriage. If she failed in this, too, she'd confirm still further what a complete disappointment she was to him as a daughter. He wouldn't blame Jim, in part, for poor financial management. The responsibility for the company's collapse would be hers and hers alone.

Restlessly she pushed the covers aside and swung her legs out of bed. She looked at the distance between it and the dressing-table. Then, slowly, she slipped off the bed and walked determinedly towards it. She was trying to prove something to herself, but not even her tenacious will could push her stamina further than its limits. She sat down wearily, dropping her head in her hands.

She looked up as she heard voices, one the nurse's, the other a resolute baritone she recognised immediately, despite the fact that it was pitched too low to carry distinctly. She glanced round for her wrap, conscious suddenly of the skimpy cut of her nightgown, as Kirk came into the room.

She felt his gaze take her in, reminding her that she was a woman. It was hard enough to forget her femininity when she was with him, without facing him wearing an insubstantial slip of silk and lace.

'I hope you feel as good as you look,' he began, his dark eyes mocking her slightly heightened colour.

'I only wish I was well enough to go home,' she said, her voice taut.

'That'll take a while yet,' Kirk reminded her. 'You had a very lucky escape.'

'I know,' she said briefly.

He moved away from the foot of the bed and went over to the window that looked over the hospital grounds. He stood there for a moment and then turned back to face her, his manner, as it so often was with her, crisp and authoritative.

'When you leave here you're coming back to me. You'll need convalescent care for several weeks, but I should think you'll be strong enough to attend the Accounting Institute's annual dinner with me. That will ease you into acting the part of my wife again before Bob comes over from the States.'

'If you think I'm ever living with you again, I can

tell you now, I'm not,' Imogen said emphatically, getting hurriedly to her feet.

She put a hand out to the dressing-table to steady herself.

'You ought to be in bed,' he said, crossing the room to her.

She took a step away from him.

'I'm not a complete invalid,' she said, refusing his assistance.

She felt shaky enough without his closeness or his touch to disturb her further. His dominating height, the square width of his shoulders and the ruthless cut of his suit, that did no more than suggest his agile strength, increased her sense of insecurity.

He waived the point with a faintly sardonic lift of his brows and she walked towards the bed unaided, biting her lip as she sank down on it, unable to conceal that to move still pained her. Ignoring his tacit agreement not to touch her, Kirk lifted her feet on to the bed. Leaning over her he said, his voice a shade harsh,

'You're coming back to me when you leave here, so let's not turn this into a discussion session. I've already arranged for someone to live in so you won't be alone during the day.'

'Then you can cancel it.'

Kirk straightened up and said,

'I thought you were anxious to leave hospital.'

'I am.'

'Well, there's no way your doctor will agree to your being discharged by Thursday of next week, once he knows you're going back to an empty flat.'

'I could be out of here by the end of next week?' she queried quickly, her eyes kindling with hope.

'That's up to you.'

There was a short silence. The choices she had were very narrow. She couldn't arrange for live-in help herself—there simply wasn't the money for that. And yet she had to be out of hospital because of the business. She might have guessed he'd use her accident as a way of hemming her in.

Kirk studied her and then asked, his voice a shade clipped despite its smooth-edged irony,

'Is the prospect of living under the same roof again so daunting? What is it exactly you're afraid of in coming back to me?'

'I'm not afraid of anything,' she lied, avoiding the directness of his eyes. 'I'm just not sure what you want from me.'

'Why don't you tell me what you're really thinking?' he asked, a curt mockery in his voice. 'You're wondering if the arrangement once you come back to me is for separate rooms. Well, you needn't worry. I've never forced myself on a woman yet. A bed partner isn't a problem; the Transit International contract is. Once that goes through, if you still want a divorce, I won't contest it. Meanwhile, if we sleep together it will be by your invitation.'

'Then you'll be waiting a long time,' Imogen said coldly, angry to find she was blushing and understanding only too well his implication.

She'd already shown him she wasn't physically immune to him. His confidence that he need take not one step more than necessary because eventually she'd come to him, was stirring her to swift annoyance. He didn't love her, but he found her attractive enough that if she weakened he'd gain the usual masculine satisfaction from seducing her. She put a hand up to her head, her eyes darkening a little.

'You're tired,' Kirk said. 'I'll leave you to get some rest. We can make the arrangements for when you want me to pick you up later.'

'You must think I'm cheap, if you suppose I'll come back to you for the reasons you've suggested,' she said with bitter defiance, pain tautening her features.

'I'd call it practical. You're intelligent enough to see the advantages work both ways. You need looking after and I've already told you my motives for wanting you back.'

'You'd do anything for money, wouldn't you?' she said contemptuously.

'I learned the value of it young,' he reminded her.

Imogen turned her head away. The letter she had left face down on the covers slipped to the floor with a faint rustle. Kirk stooped to pick it up.

'Give me that!' she said quickly, her voice sharp with alarm.

His dark, analytic eyes considered her a moment before he unfolded the sheet of paper. He did no more than scan the first few lines.

'So you're being threatened with legal action,' he commented, before tossing the letter dismissively on the bed.

'New Radiance is nothing to do with you.'

'It is if you're declared insolvent,' he told her, before adding with clipped sarcasm, 'That would look good, wouldn't it, to have my wife's company wound up through financial incompetence just as the Transit International contract comes up?'

'The company won't be wound up,' she said tersely.

She closed her eyes for an instant against the knives of pain, sensing Kirk's gaze on her as she fought to regain her show of courage. He took hold of her wrist, and she started a little at the warm, firm pressure of his touch.

'I said before I was prepared to offer you a loan,' he told her, his tone gentler. 'That offer still stands.'

'The last thing I want is to be indebted to you.'

Kirk released her.

'I thought the last thing you wanted was to see New Radiance fold,' he said, moving away a little. She didn't answer and he went on, 'I can't afford to allow you to go out of business, not now. So I suggest you tell that fool of a brother of yours that once I've seen the balance sheets for the last financial year we'll come to some kind of agreement.'

There was a long pause and then Imogen said,

'I'll speak to him about it. And now, if you've no other terms you want to set out, I'd like to get some sleep.'

He came and stood over her, studying her in silence for a moment before asking, with an abrupt change of topic,

'Has your father been to see you yet?'

Imogen looked at him sharply, as though startled by the question.

'My father hasn't seen me or spoken to me since we split up,' she said, her voice constrained and with a catch of emotion in it.

'Do you want me to phone him?'

'No!' she said fiercely.

The rift between her and her father had left her feeling hurt and confused. Kirk's sympathy was threatening to break down her pretended indifference. She wouldn't let him see how very isolated she felt, and especially not now when she was so completely in his power.

'Just what was it you and your father rowed over?' he asked.

'My walking out on you, among other things. He doesn't like the thought of a divorce in the family.'

'You're not divorced yet,' he reminded her.

Imogen's spirit rose in rebellion against his complete assurance. He was so utterly accustomed to twisting life to his will, he couldn't believe she would stand out against him, refuse his terms. And yet circumstances, or maybe it was fate, seemed to be forcing her back to him. Why did everything always have to work out to his advantage?

She didn't answer him and he bent to kiss her. She tensed a little against the pillows. There had been too much between them for even the most casual physical contact to be innocuous. His broad shoulders as he leaned close to her came between her and the light. She felt his lips brush her cheek, the slight roughness of his jaw grazing her face. His touch disturbed her.

'Call me later in the week when you've spoken to your doctor,' he said as he walked to the door.

She didn't restate that she had no intention of leaving the hospital with him. She couldn't seem to find the energy. Turning her head away, she heard the door click to behind him.

Jim stopped by at the hospital late in the evening to collect the letter he'd left with her.

'Kirk was here this afternoon,' she began.

'I would have thought you could have done without seeing him,' he remarked as he sat down on the bed.

'He's offered to come up with a loan.'

'Tell him he can keep it. We don't need his money.'

'Jim, be realistic. We desperately need the money.'

'You mean you told him we were having cash-flow problems?' he demanded, a note of accusation in his voice.

'No, of course not. He happened to see the letter, but even if he hadn't, he's guessed all along that things aren't going well.'

'You didn't agree to accept a loan from him, did you?' Jim asked in annoyed disbelief.

'I said I'd put it to you. I don't like the idea much either, but when it comes to business, Kirk's got the Midas touch. I want to save the company. I'll do anything for that.'

He levelled a finger at her as he said emphatically,

'I'm not working with Kirk.'

'You wouldn't be. All he wants to do is look at the balance sheets. There's no question of his being involved in the management of the business.'

'There's just no way I'm having your husband scrutinising the company accounts,' Jim said harshly. 'You don't think he wants to look at them for nothing, do you? We won't get that money unless he has a say in things, and his ideas and mine are completely opposed.'

'Well, yours haven't been too bright of late,' she pointed out with unthinking bluntness. She broke off and said regretfully, 'I didn't mean that.'

'Didn't you? Kirk's really won you over, hasn't he?'

'No. I'm just trying to be practical. I won't let New Radiance fold.'

'So you work with me for all this time and now, just because the going gets a bit tough, you start siding with Kirk against me!' he snapped, exploding into anger.

'Don't be so ridiculous! It's not a question of siding with anyone.'

Jim laughed shortly, cutting across her sarcastically as he said,

'And they always say blood's thicker than water. It's certainly not true in this case. I might have guessed that when it came to it you'd back him against me.'

'Well, that's a good joke! I'm not siding with Kirk against you. I never have done and I'm certainly not now. How can you think it? I don't know what's got into you that you're taking it like this. You know how I care about you. You're my brother.'

He flung the hand she had put on his arm away.

'I'm your half-brother. It seems to make a difference.'

There was a sudden appalled silence, then Imogen said in a hushed voice,

'What did you say?'

'Nothing,' Jim said quickly. 'I didn't mean it. I was angry. Forget it.'

She rested her head, that was throbbing sickeningly, back against the pillows. Her voice was shocked into calmness.

'You said you were my half-brother.' She thought of her father's barely concealed dislike of her and suddenly everything slotted into place. 'Dad's not my real father, is he? And he's known it all along. That's why he's hated me. That's why he hasn't even visited me in hospital.'

'No,' Jim denied swiftly. 'It's not true.'

Imogen ignored his denial.

'How did you know when I didn't?' she demanded.

'He didn't answer and she repeated the question, her voice notched a shade higher.

'How did you know?'

'I heard Mum and Dad rowing,' he admitted in sudden capitulation. 'God, Imogen, I didn't mean to hurt you. I was worried about the business and . . . ' He trailed off, his eyes narrowed.

'But you must have known for years,' she said slowly.

'Yes, I've known, but it didn't matter. You're still my sister. I still care about you, Imogen. I'm sorry, I should never . . . '

'Do you know who my father is?' she asked, cutting across him.

'No,' he said briefly, before continuing miserably, 'I don't know anything beyond what I heard all those years ago. It wasn't long before Mum died, and you weren't much more than five. I thought you never need know. I never meant you to know'.

There was a long, empty silence and then Imogen said quietly,

'Don't feel bad. It's not your fault, and you couldn't

have been a better brother even if we had shared the same father.'

Jim stood up and moved away from the bed, his hands in his pockets, his shoulders slumped.

'Look,' he said, his voice low and constrained, 'just give me the chance to get the company on its feet my way, will you?'

He turned back to her, unable to find the words he wanted immediately. 'Don't bring Kirk into this. I swear to you, I won't let you down.'

Imogen nodded, her throat tightening in her refusal to give way to tears.

It was some time later before Jim left. She'd told him she'd reject Kirk's offer of a loan, but she wasn't thinking of the company now. She was thinking of Kirk. She'd never had his love. Now, if he knew the truth about her she wouldn't even have his respect. A wife who didn't even know the identity of her father wasn't much of an asset. This, more than Lydia, marked the complete end of their relationship.

CHAPTER FIVE

OVER the next few days, the truth of what Jim had told Imogen about her father sank deeper. At first she had wondered if it was effect of shock that had made her take the news so calmly. She should be shattered, the edifices that had supported the notions of who she was smashed, leaving her adrift with no clear sense of identity. But she wasn't. Instead, all she was left with was a sober realisation of how very alone she was, and a cold apprehension of how Kirk would view her if he ever learned that her sterling backround wasn't what it seemed. She flinched at the thought of seeing contempt in his eyes. It was only because their marriage was over that she would never have to tell him.

She saw now that she could go back to him until the contract was signed. Everything was finally over between them. Surely there could be no risk in living with him again, when she knew that he had only to learn the truth for him to despise her as much as her father did? She had to be out of hospital to stave off the company collapsing. Her options seemed suddenly very narrow and very clear.

Peter looked in to see her the following Monday.

'How are you doing?' he asked as he drew up a chair beside her.

'Ok,' she told him with a forced smile. 'In fact, I'm going home on Thursday.'

'Thursday,' he repeated. 'That's great. I thought you'd have to stay in longer than that.'

'Yes, well, there have been conditions attached,' she admitted.

'I suppose you've had to say you won't be tempted to drive or to go into work,' Peter said. 'Still, you shouldn't need to, not with your brother in the business.'

'Peter . . .' She paused, then said quietly, 'I know you won't understand this, but when I leave hospital I'm going back to Kirk.'

'You're what?' he exclaimed. 'Well, you're damned right, I don't understand it.'

'Believe me, I do have my reasons for going back to him. We're having a trial period and then Kirk's agreed we'll divorce amicably, or at least as amicably as possible.'

'You just astound me at times. You know it's over between the two of you.'

'I don't need that pointed out,' she said, running a distraught hand through her hair. 'I'm sorry. I know this is hard for you to understand.'

'Well,' Peter said brusquely, 'this makes a decision easier for me.'

'What decision?' she asked uncomprehendingly.

'I've been offered a transfer to our office in Montreal. I didn't know whether I should take it or not.'

'What are you trying to do? Make me feel guilty?'

'It seems to me I don't make you feel anything at all.' He stood up and said sardonically, 'I'll send you a post-card.'

'Peter, don't let's finish this way,' she said swiftly.

'I'm not prepared to hang around till you get your life sorted out. When you finally make the break from your husband, get in touch.'

He didn't kiss her goodbye, nor did he pause at the doorway. It occurred to her that it was another relationship she had failed with, and yet she wasn't altogether sorry it was over between them. If she couldn't have Kirk in her life she didn't want anyone.

Sometimes it seemed as though she'd been lonely

every day since they'd split up, as if she'd never relate to another man again. That was absurd. If the accident hadn't left her so weak and drained she wouldn't feel this way.

The orderly routine of the hospital gave her plenty of time to think through what she was doing. The prospect of going home with Kirk made her apprehensive. Going back to him with none of the hostility between them resolved, and now with a secret to keep from him as well, meant living with an edge of tension she suddenly wasn't sure she could handle.

The staff nurse seemed surprised that, although Imogen had been so anxious to leave hospital, she showed no excitement about going home. Kirk had visited the hospital regularly and had an easy pleasant manner with the nurses. To the outward observer it looked as if she had a good marriage and a caring husband. The irony stung more than a little.

It was evening when he came to collect her. She was glad to take his arm as they walked along the corridor. Kirk modified his purposeful stride to her cautious pace. She hated this unfamiliar dependence on him.

'I've parked very near the exit,' he told her. 'You won't have far to walk.'

He held the passenger door open for her and, reluctantly, she got in. As he started the engine he said, 'I've got an *au pair* to live in. She's from Belgium. She wants to work in the tourist industry, so this is a way of improving her English.'

'What's her name?' asked Imogen.

'Jeanne Anthoni.'

'When does she start?'

'Why? Are you afraid of even one night alone with me?' he asked.

'We had an agreement,' she reminded him.

'Which I intend keeping to,' he said, his voice a

shade harsh as he pulled out from the hospital drive on to the main road.

The silence between them lengthened. Imogen broke it by saying,

'You didn't tell me when Jeanne was to start.'

'She's at home now. She moved in this afternoon.'

'You could have told me that straight away,' Imogen pointed out sharply.

'Maybe I just wanted to test your reactions.'

'Well, now you have. I'd never have agreed to live under the same roof with you again if it hadn't been for the accident.'

'Don't worry,' Kirk said tersely. 'I have no illusions on that score.'

They completed the drive in silence for the most part. For Imogen, it was stirring memories she would have rather left undisturbed. When she had walked out on Kirk she had intended never going back to him. Now, as they drove along the quiet, tree-lined road, she was reminded of that resolution.

Kirk swung the Mercedes into the circular drive of their house. It was modern, built on attractive, clean lines and with a wide frontage. Once she had thought of it as home. Now it seemed like his house, and his alone.

Jeanne must have seen the car draw up, for she came to the front door. In her late teens, she was a slim, dark-haired girl with large, rather anxious eyes. Imogen was glad she was there. Having to make conversation with her and concentrate on her strongly accented English diverted her thoughts from Kirk.

'Would you like me to unpack for you, Mrs Cameron?' Jeanne asked as Kirk carried her suitcases into the hall.

It occurred to Imogen that, with all her possessions at the flat, her bedroom would look strangely unoccupied.

'Thank you, but I can manage,' she said quickly.

'Then I'll go and see to the dinner.'

Kirk waited till Jeanne had gone through to the kitchen before saying,

'The journey's tired you. I'll carry you upstairs and you can lie down till the meal's ready.'

'I don't need to be carried,' she protested, a faint note of alarm in her voice..

He ignored her, sweeping her into his arms as if she were no heavier than a child, before mounting the stairs.

'Put me down!' she insisted, pushing an angry hand against his substantial chest.

It was true that she did feel almost shaky with fatigue, but she didn't want to be reminded of her vulnerability. Nor did she need this parody of their homecoming following their honeymoon.

'Stop being so stubborn,' Kirk said shortly.

He pushed open the door of the double bedroom which once, it seemed a long time ago, they had shared. For an instant, memories crowded in on her, robbing her of the will to fight him. He strode over to the bed and stood with her in his arms, looking down at her. His dark eyes, implacable and penetrating, searched hers. She was conscious of the ruthlessness of his cheekbones, the hard line of his jaw, of the fact that he was still her husband.

Then he laid her on the bed. She pulled back instinctively against the pillows, kicking her shoes off and drawing her feet up towards her. The defensiveness of her movements was not lost on Kirk.

He strolled over to the window and, with his hands in his pockets, gazed out on to the street. To Imogen he seemed completely relaxed, while she was cramped with tension, unable to blot out thoughts of the nights she had spent here with him before they had become estranged.

He crossed over to the chest of drawers and took out a turquoise silk nightgown. Coming towards the bed he asked,

'Do you need any help to undress?'

'No!' she said fiercely, almost snatching the night-gown from him, before demanding, 'How did this get here, anyway?'

'I took the liberty of fetching some of your clothes for you from your flat. You remember giving me the key when you asked me to turn the water off?'

He succeeded in shading the word 'liberty' with faint irony, and Imogen gave him a cold look of dislike. She thought of him packing her intimate belongings, his hands carelessly touching her lingerie, and it was as if in doing so he had already assumed the rights of a husband.

'If I embarrass you,' he said with deft sarcasm, 'I'll go out while you undress.'

'You don't,' she lied as she slithered off the bed. 'It's just that I prefer privacy.'

Kirk gave her a faint, sardonic nod as he conceded the point and then went out. She waited a moment and then, hearing his quick, sure step on the stairs, she reached up behind her neck to unfasten the zip of her dress. It ran a short way before jamming. Impatiently she pulled at it. This was all she needed! She struggled with it a moment longer before going on to the landing to call Jeanne. Kirk was coming upstairs with her case.

She hesitated momentarily, then she said with a touch of defiance,

'My zip's jammed. Will you undo it for me?'

She wasn't sure just which of them she was trying to prove something to. If she was going to stay here she had to establish her independence from him.

'Sure,' he said, joining her on the landing and putting a hand on her shoulder.

'I can't think how it jammed,' she said, striving to keep her voice normal.

'The material's very fine. It's caught in the zip.'

He swept her hair away from her neck. She took a steadying breath and waited for him to free her. She was aware of him standing close to her and of the hard strength of his build.

'That's it,' he said as the zip slid down to her waist.

'Thanks,' she said, turning immediately so that she was out of his reach.

She preceded him into her room and sat down, hoping he wouldn't notice how tremulous she felt. Kirk set her case down.

'I'll give you a shout when dinner's ready,' he said as he went out.

Imogen slipped off her dress. It troubled her to discover how tired the journey home had made her. In the hospital she had somehow assumed that, despite what the doctor had told her, she'd notice an almost immediate improvement once she was home. At this rate, just when would she be able to get back to work?

She must have slept, for the next thing she knew the room was dark and someone was tapping at the door. For a moment she couldn't think where she was, and then Jeanne came in.

'Dinner's ready, Mrs Cameron. Would you like me to bring you a tray upstairs?'

If she said yes, Kirk would construe it that she lacked the courage to face him.

'No, I'll come down.'

She got up and pulled on her wrap. She sashed it firmly, and in bare feet walked over to the dressing-table. As she crossed the deep-piled rug something sharp dug into her foot. Bending down, she ran her hand over it to see what had stabbed her and she found close to the backing a diamond ear-ring set round with small rubies.

For an instant she stared at it, refusing to come to the obvious conclusion. It didn't have to be Lydia's. Perhaps Jeanne had dropped it, but Jeanne, she was certain, wasn't wearing ear-rings, and besides, she was unlikely to own any jewellery of such value. Imogen tightened her hand around it, unable to evade the truth. The ear-ring was Lydia's. It couldn't have been dropped by anyone else, and that could only mean that she had been sleeping with Kirk in this room, perhaps as recently as the day before.

The reality rocked the core of her inner composure. She knew that Kirk was still involved with Lydia, but knowing it hadn't prepared her in any way for experiencing the shock and anger of realising he had slept with her here in this room, in this bed. Remembering the nights she had lain beside him was like a knife-thrust of pain. How could he have made love to Lydia in the same bed where he had taken such fierce possession of her night after night?

She sat down at the dressing-table. This was a hurt that went too deep to be soothed by tears. She clenched her hand more tightly till the metal of the ear-ring dug into her palm, hating Kirk for his indifference towards her with a furious intensity. It was some while later before she went downstairs, outwardly at least, austerely calm.

She had no intention of confronting Kirk with the ear-ring. There could be no explanation for it being in her bedroom other than the one she'd arrived at. And she couldn't bear to hear him confirm with uncaring curtness that he and Lydia had shared the bed where he had once slept with her. She was newly convalescent and her emotions were very near the surface. If she as much as mentioned Lydia to Kirk tonight she knew she would break down into a storm of angry tears.

He was in the lounge watching the end of the nine

o'clock news. As Imogen appeared in the doorway he switched the set to standby.

'I didn't realise it was so late,' she began, her voice cool.

'Jeanne held the meal back. It seemed a shame to wake you.'

She wondered if it had been Jeanne who had looked in on her while she slept, or him. An angry defiance was lending her the false illusion of strength, helping her to convince herself that she didn't care who he was involved with. It was the business that was important to her, though even with that at risk, she wasn't sure she could stay here now. And yet what alternative did she have?

'You're very quiet,' he commented, giving her a speculative glance.

'There's nothing much to say,' she said shortly.

She noted the alterations in the room since she had left him. The new wallpaper, sofa and armchairs made it seem even more as if she didn't belong in this house. Evidently, Lydia didn't like her taste.

Kirk watched her and then commented, 'The place was done over a few weeks back. All my electrical equipment was stolen and there was quite a lot of damage downstairs. If you don't like any of the decorations you can alter them.'

His explanation for the changes reduced just a little the angry desolation she felt, though not by much.

'I shan't be here long enough for that,' she said stonily. 'In fact, I don't know I intend staying at all.'

Jeanne came in to say that the meal was ready and Kirk said,

'We'll talk about this later.'

Jeanne joined them for dinner. Her presence meant the conversation kept safely to neutral topics. It wasn't until the meal was over and Imogen was left alone with Kirk again that the façade of normality showed clearly as being false.

'More wine?' Kirk asked. She shook her head and he went on, 'I didn't get champagne. I thought it might look too much like a celebration.'

'A celebration of victory?' she asked cuttingly, before adding with a touch of bitterness, 'Well, why not? After all, you have won. I'm back with you again.'

He brought his hand down on the table so the wine in his glass lurched.

'No, I don't look on this as a victory,' he said angrily. 'Your being well enough to come home was the celebration. When you're fully recovered, then we'll have the champagne.'

'And what will there be to celebrate then?' she asked, adding with chill sarcasm, 'I forgot. Of course, then there will be the signing of the contract to celebrate. That's if I stay that long.'

She pushed back her chair and stood up, throwing her napkin on the table as she went to pass him.

Kirk waited till she was level with him before reaching out and taking hold of her by the arm.

'I let you walk out on me before,' he said, his dark eyes stabbing hers, 'because I thought maybe you needed some space to sort out your feelings. Now you're not strong so I won't push you, but I warn you, I'm not going to let you evade me for ever and I'm not letting you go until I've got what I want.'

She snatched her arm away and didn't answer. Deliberately, she resisted the impulse to quicken her pace as she left the room. She wouldn't give him the satisfaction of knowing it was flight.

For a long time before sleep came Imogen lay gazing at the darkened ceiling. She mustn't think that Lydia had slept beside Kirk in this bed—the thought was unendurable. Her relationship with Kirk was over. She must keep reminding herself of that. What he did and who he slept with were of no concern to her.

She turned her cheek against the pillow. If only Graeme were still alive! She hadn't known what it meant to be hurt and used by a man till she had fallen in love with Kirk. How much simpler it would have been if she could have gone on believing that she had been in love with Graeme. But Kirk had destroyed that illusion.

She thought back to when they had first met. Graeme had made her feel valued and loved, and she had known almost immediately that she wanted to spend her whole life with him. Graeme, an engineer with an oil company, was being sent out to Qatar for six months, and as soon as he came back they planned to marry. That last evening together he'd wanted her to sleep with him and she had gently refused him. And then the news had come of his death, and shock and grief had been mingled with the now irrectifiable guilt she felt because she had drawn back from physical unity with him. Not till a full year later, when she was married to Kirk, did she understand the reason why she had drawn back. She hadn't been in love with him, not as she was with Kirk, who only had to touch her sexually for her to respond to him.

At last she drifted into troubled sleep, and into a nightmare that had all the garish reality of a Cinemascope film. She was with Kirk in the study and they were arguing. The contract he wanted with Transit International was agreed. To celebrate he intended taking Lydia away for a short break abroad. Despair engulfed her as she sought for some way to hold on to their ruined marriage, knowing even as she did that it was impossible. Tears stung her eyes as Kirk told her brusquely that they were finished. He had no further use for her.

In an agony of heartbreak she turned from the room and ran through the hall and outside to where her car was parked in the drive. She started the engine and, unseeing, pulled out on to the road, noticing too late the lorry that was coming towards her. Its massive cab blotted out the light, filling the whole windscreen. Again came the paralysing certainty of death, an overwhelming terror. She gave a frantic cry and woke with a violent start to hear her scream echoing in the darkness.

She sat up, trying to push back the horror of the nightmare that was still frighteningly real. She was trembling and the silence of the lonely bedroom oppressed her. Unsteadily, she got out of bed. Her head was starting to throb dully, a prelude to one of the blinding headaches that the doctor had warned her could persist for some time. She went over to her dressing-table to look for her tablets before remembering she had left them downstairs.

Shrugging on her wrap, she went on to the landing. The window on to the staircase was uncurtained and there was enough wan moonlight for her to see quite clearly. If she switched on the light she ran the risk of waking Kirk. She bit her lip against the intensifying rhythm of fierce pain as she went into the lounge for her pain-killers. Shaking a couple of tablets into her hand, she went into the kitchen and switched on the harsh strip-lighting.

She reached up to one of the cupboards to get a glass, her wide sleeve brushing against one of the glass storage jars on the work surface. It fell on the tiles with a splintering crash, sending fragments of glass darting across the floor. For an instant Imogen stared at it in dismay, and then, pressing the back of her hand against her mouth to stifle tears of vexation, she stooped down to pick up the larger fragments.

'What on earth are you doing?'

She started and looked up sharply as Kirk's voice came from the doorway. He was standing there in a robe, the dark hair of his deep chest which showed between the lapels, and his naked, hard-muscled legs, evidence that on hearing the crash he had come downstairs immediately. The images of the nightmare were still sharp-etched enough for this unexpected confrontation to produce a chaotic upsurge of emotion in her.

She swallowed hard and said, her voice within a notch of breaking,

'I wanted some water to take my tablets with.'

She flinched and closed her eyes as the pain tautened unbearably. Kirk was across the room to her in an instant, taking her by the shoulders as he pulled her into his arms. She couldn't think of resisting. For a moment, all the hostility she felt towards him was gone. He represented strength and protection, and she turned her face into his hard shoulder as his arms tightened round her.

'My head aches so dreadfully,' she said, her voice sharpened by pain.

He held her a moment longer then crossed over to the sink, ran a glass of water, and handed it to her. She opened her fist and swallowed the tablets.

'I'm sorry about all the broken glass,' she said.

'Forget it,' he answered, putting an arm round her and leading her into the lounge.

She sat down on the nearest armchair, dropping her head in her hands.

'You're very tense,' he observed.

The pain was still agonisingly acute, but it no longer so completely overrode her recollection of the barrier of differences between them.

'I had a nightmare. It upset me,' she said briefly.

'It would help if you could talk about it,' he said as he perched on the arm of her chair.

That was the one thing she couldn't do.

'It was about the car crash,' she told him, hoping that was explanation enough and bowing her head as the radials of pain intensified again.

She caught her breath as she felt his hands on her shoulders, easing the collar of her wrap lower. She went to pull away, but he restrained her.

'Try to relax,' he ordered as he started to massage the tension out of her taut muscles.

Imogen knew she should protest, but the firmness of his touch was making her headache deaden a little, leaving her pliant, relaxed, unresisting.

'Does it help at all?' he asked.

She nodded, closing her eyes, feeling his capable hands caressing her bare skin in a way that was pleasantly hypnotic, dangerously sensual. She gave a faint sigh. When he touched her like this she seemed to have no will at all. He slid the ribbon-fine straps of her nightgown gently over her shoulders so that his hands could travel over a wider area.

'What happened?' he asked. 'Did you dream the crash was happening all over again?'

'In a sort of a way,' she admitted unthinkingly.

'How was that?'

Kirk's question reminded her of all the bitterness in their relationship which her nightmare had highlighted with such cruel realism. She realised suddenly how much she had relaxed against him. For an instant she had forgotten about Lydia, and how empty their being together was, despite the fact that they were still married. She wouldn't give him the satisfaction of reading the obvious meaning behind her nightmare. She hunted quickly for a a convincing lie and couldn't find one.

'Don't pull away,' he said. 'You're tensing up again.'

His close, pressing hands slid caressingly over the slope of her shoulders and this time she recognised the betraying warm softness that ebbed through her for what it was. His touch was making her ache to respond to him. The treacherousness of her senses angered her. She ought to reassert her independence, move away, instead of flirting with danger. He felt nothing for her. To allow him to seduce her would be a further triumph for him, and she had no doubt he'd find the challenge amusing. A dart of pain across her left temple made her delay rejecting his closeness.

'You should have come to me instead of coming downstairs on your own,' he told her. 'You might have fallen.'

'I didn't want to wake you,' she said.

'You still haven't told me what the nightmare was about,' he reminded her.

His hands slid down her arms, sending ripples of yielding warmth through her. It was a wayward moment. She couldn't trust it. She mustn't trust it. The reality of day would show it as illusory as her dream. Kirk pulled her gently to him so she lay in the crook of his arm.

She saw the strong cords of his neck, the way the robe gaped a little, showing his hard, muscled chest. It flashed into her mind that it was over a year since he had last made love to her. A sudden loneliness for him made her briefly want to forget about the irredeemable flaws in their relationship. She clenched her fist as she imagined sliding her hand between the lapels of his robe, feeling his warm skin under her exploring fingers. She knew that a part of her wanted him to take her, for him to erase the empty feeling of being alone which the nightmare had evoked, in that crescendo of coming together. But it wasn't an answer.

'I dreamed about Graeme,' she said abruptly.

She went to pull away, but his hands tightened on her arms.

'Tell me.'

There was something in his voice that told her he meant to be obeyed. She had expected her confession to bring an immediate barrier of restraint between them, and that he would release her.

'I can't,' she said in a constrained voice.

He tilted her chin towards him, forcing her to meet his dark eyes.

'Tell me,' he insisted. 'You're obviously deeply troubled or you wouldn't have had such a disturbing dream. Bottling up what you feel isn't going to make what's upsetting you go away.'

'You wouldn't understand,' Imogen faltered in alarm, dropping her gaze.

The pressure of his fingers came hotly on to her skin. She tried to subdue her awareness of his lean male build.

'Try me, anyway,' he said, his voice a shade harsh.

'All right,' she conceded, breaking away from him with an effort of will and drawing her wrap protectively around her. Kirk didn't prompt her, but she sensed his eyes on her, those dark, shrewd eyes that had all the sharpness of a hunter. Whatever she said now had to be convincing.

Lifting her chin, she began at last,

'I dreamt I was arguing with Graeme. He was saying I didn't love him and whatever I did, he just turned away from me.'

She stopped abruptly. It had been simple enough to substitute Graeme's name when she was recounting her nightmare. She hadn't realised that by doing so she had inadvertently admitted she was aware there had been flaws in her relationship with Graeme. Kirk still believed her feelings for Graeme were unaltered. She was determined he should go on believing that.

Turning to confront him, she said, her voice low and full of hostility as she tried to redeem her unthinking mistake,

'I suppose you find that quite amusing. After all, you've taken great pains to point out that the fact that Graeme and I weren't lovers was a sign there was something very lacking in our relationship.'

'I don't find it amusing at all,' he said, and the quiet sincerity of his voice made her glance at him in surprise.

She hadn't expected either understanding or concern from him and, now that she had them, she wasn't sure how to react. It was as though, without one blow, he had shattered her stout defences against him, so that she stood there with no armour of hostility to keep him at arm's length.

'It was all so vivid,' she said, reverting back to honesty, her voice a shade unsteady as the full horror of the nightmare returned. 'And then the dream became confused with the car crash.'

Kirk came swiftly towards her, taking her in his arms and holding her close. She closed her eyes, turning her cheek into his shoulder and feeling the slight roughness of his robe as her fingers pressed against his back. Her headache had eased and the cessation of pain brought in its wake a sweeping fatigue.

She didn't protest as, gently, he lifted her in his arms and carried her out of the lounge and up the stairs. She saw that the sash of her wrap had loosened so that it barely covered the enticingly low line of her nightgown, and as Kirk pushed open the door of her bedroom she tried to draw the lapel nearer to her throat.

'You're not shy with me, are you?' Kirk mocked. 'After all I've seen you in a lot less.'

She flashed him a glance of resentment but didn't answer. The pain-killers were starting to take effect. She recognised the slight drifting sensation they induced that wasn't unpleasant so long as she didn't struggle against it. Wearily, she rested her head against his shoulder in a gesture of capitulation.

She felt him lay her on the bed and the soothing dip of the mattress as he leaned over her. She wondered if she imagined the brush of his lips against her cheek. He went to the door and her confused senses recorded, with a surge of alarm, that he was leaving her and that she was slipping back into a shadowy world that still held the fear of her nightmare.

'Kirk——' she began, her voice low and pleading.

Her eyes, darkened slightly with pain and apprehension, met his. She hadn't realised what reassurance she had found in being close to him. She needed his arms round her, the comfort of his hard-muscled body next to hers, the firmness of his personality. Lydia and her damaged pride no longer seemed to matter. Pain, and the tablets she had taken, were making cool rationality recede, leaving only an elemental need not to be alone in the empty night.

'Please,' she whispered, 'don't leave me. Not just yet.'

Kirk came towards her, sliding on to the bed and drawing her into his arms. Her heart thudding at the physical contact, she slid her fingers up around his neck, scarcely aware of what she was doing or that she had again murmured his name. She had the impression she was falling, as gently he leaned forward, pressing her back against the pillows, his body covering hers. Her hand slid between his lapels as she turned her cheek against his chest, finding the strength and warmth of contact she had yearned for. The tortured way he muttered her name as she moved against him and the tremor of restraint in his close, pressing arms made no impact on the surface of her consciousness.

CHAPTER SIX

IMOGEN awoke to a feeling of infinite peace that seemed to pervade her whole being. It was morning. She ran her hand alongside her over the smoothness of the sheets, dreamily relaxed, then she stiffened suddenly as she realised that Kirk lay beside her. The warmth of his naked body so close to hers in the intimacy of the crumpled covers sent a shock wave rippling through her. His hair was dark against the pillow as he slept, one arm flung forwards, towards her on the bed. It was obvious from the way he was turned towards her, the disordered sheets showing the tanned curve of his broad chest, that she had slept with his arm thrown across her, the way she always had after they had made love.

She gave a gasp of dismay as realisation hit her. The treacherous unreality of the night had gone, and with it the illusory closeness she had felt with him. He had seduced her in the same bed where he had lain with Lydia. She couldn't remember the intimate details of the night, but the evidence of their lovemaking was clear enough.

Self-contempt flared up and then turned into an outraged hatred of him. Last night she had been weak, confused, vulnerable. She hadn't known what she was doing. But *he* had. He had implied that his seduction of her would be effortless, and it had been. Perhaps, she thought bitterly, he *should* have bought champagne for them that evening. The spoils were to the victor and, in one night, he had succeeded not only in getting her back into the matrimonial home, but into the matrimonial bed.

She shrank away from him, about to slide out of bed. The knowledge that, perhaps as close as a single night ago, Lydia had slept beside him made her feel physically sick. The movement wakened him and drowsily he pulled her back towards him. Her shattered senses recorded the dominating power of his naked body, the warmth of his lean thighs, the hard muscles of his chest. In a frenzy of apprehension she struck her hand against him.

'Don't you dare touch me!' she cried.

Hardness and comprehension came into his dark eyes. His jawline tightened to ruthlessness as his hands swiftly caught both her wrists, rendering her helpless.

'Let go of me,' she gasped.

Kirk pushed her roughly down against the pillows. Her breathing was quickened with alarm as he leant over her. She was conscious of the provocative rise and fall of her breasts in the silky nightgown and with a furious effort she tried to wrench free, but her strength was useless against his.

'You didn't find me so repellent last night,' he said angrily, his dark eyes burning hers. 'So what's changed things this morning? Or can you only act like a woman when you're half drugged?'

A sickening dizziness was sweeping her. So he *had* taken her last night. He saw that she had paled slightly and he released her with a suddenness that held contempt. He studied her a moment and then he laughed shortly.

'Let me set your mind at rest, since it's obvious what's bothering you. We didn't make love last night, though you tempted me enough. I'm not inhuman, Imogen. Next time, unless you're prepared to take the consequences, don't come to me all soft and yielding, because I may not be quite so controlled.'

He flung the covers aside and got out of bed. For an instant she took in the raw sexuality of his male body, and then she swiftly averted her eyes as, shrugging on his robe, he left the room. Shakily she sat up, instinctively shrinking away from the warm imprint of the sheets where he had lain beside her. She must have been mad to have agreed to come back to him. She couldn't understand it, but somehow the enmity between them held an undercurrent of latent sexuality that made every encounter with him potentially dangerous.

She couldn't deny the truth. Part of her did want physical closeness with him, but not like this, not tinged with anger and bitterness. What staggered her was that when she knew he was still sleeping with Lydia he still had the power to make her conscious of an aching need for completeness with him. She ran a harassed hand through her hair and got up.

If she dressed and went downstairs now, it would mean facing Kirk over breakfast. It was cowardly to stay in her room, but for the moment, with the disordered bed reminding her of how she had spent the night in his arms, she didn't have the self-possession she needed to face him again.

She waited till she heard the sound of his car pulling away before she went downstairs. Knowing that she had a respite from his demanding personality till the evening alleviated the build-up of uneasiness. What was she doing living with him again? It was true that circumstances had her trapped, but wasn't she too compliant a victim? She left the question unanswered, as lately she had left so many about herself and her feelings for Kirk.

Jeanne was in the kitchen.

'Good morning,' she began in her formal English. 'I hope you slept well.'

Imogen coloured a little as she thought of the events

of the night before. She remembered the smashed storage jar, the innocuous evidence of what had acted as a prelude to her night with Kirk. But the fragments of glass were gone. She supposed Kirk had disposed of them. She gave the conventional polite reply to Jeanne's question and joined her at the table.

'You and Mr Cameron,' Jeanne asked, 'have you been married long?'

'Three years,' said Imogen, pouring herself some coffee.

'That's nice,' Jeanne commented, before saying, 'Your husband, he's very caring.'

It taxed Imogen to concur. She could imagine that to an outsider Kirk could well appear an enviable husband, successful, dynamic, strong. But then Jeanne didn't know about Lydia or about the Transit International contract.

She changed the tack of the conversation by asking Jeanne about her home in Bruges.

'I show you a photo,' said Jeanne as she fetched her handbag. Taking out a photo, she passed it to Imogen. 'That's my mother and father, and this is my brother and his wife and their little girl.'

'How old is she?' asked Imogen with a smile.

'She will be three in September,' Jeanne said before asking, 'You do not have any children yet?'

'No,' Imogen confirmed quickly.

Jeanne evidently mistook the slight curtness of her answer for regret, for she said tentatively, trying to be kind,

'Perhaps one day.'

Imogen resisted the temptation to say not if she could help it. Jeanne couldn't possibly guess from appearances what a farce her marriage was, and she meant well.

'Who knows?' Imogen managed amiably.

Yet curiously the idea stayed with her. As she went

through into the lounge she found herself wondering how it might have been if she had had Kirk's baby. The strange yearning the mental picture produced made her cut the speculation short. Her reaction puzzled her. Having a child wouldn't have held their marriage together. Being a single parent and trying to look after a baby and run the business would have been almost impossible. Taking a purely practical view, it would have been a disaster for her to have conceived. And yet having his child would have meant having a part of him for always. She picked up the paper impatiently and began to read.

It was only as afternoon slipped into evening and she thought of encountering Kirk again, that apprehension brought on another headache. She sat huddled on the sofa, her forehead pressed against a cushion. She had been too hard on herself, she thought, as she clenched her hands against the throbbing pain. Small wonder she had capitulated last night to the sensuous persuasion of Kirk's hands relaxing her taut shoulders. She'd submit to anything to be free from this explosion of torture.

The phone rang and she heard Jeanne go into the hall. A moment later she appeared in the doorway and asked quietly,

'It's Mr Cameron. Do you feel well enough to speak to him?'

Imogen nodded and, getting up wearily, walked into the hall and picked up the receiver.

'Imogen?' Kirk's voice on the phone sounded hard, impersonal. 'There's a problem cropped up at work so I'll be late home. I shan't be in till after ten.'

It occurred to her bitterly how nothing between them had changed. Before she'd left him he'd told her he was working late when in reality he was seeing Lydia. Presumably, he was using the same excuse now.

'All right,' she said, conscious that her voice sounded strained.

'What's wrong?' he asked curtly.

'Nothing. Another headache,' she said. 'I'll see you this evening.'

She replaced the receiver hurriedly, knowing full well the motive for her abruptness.

Jim didn't contact her over the next few days. She had assured the doctor she'd be sensible about convalescing, but the company was too close to collapsing for her to stick rigidly to that assurance. At the very least, she'd have to insist Jim come round to discuss the state of play with her. She was unable to reach him at any of the salons. Finally, she tried his home number.

'Hi,' Jim answered cheerfully. 'It's good to hear you. How are you feeling?'

'I'm fine,' she said.

'You've only just caught me. I was just off to the bank to speak to Mr Hollis about our overdraft facilities.'

'You mean we may be able to raise more money?' she asked, with a mixture of doubt and hope.

'I think we can sort something out,' Jim said confidently. 'Anyway, I'll get back to you if any snags should crop up.'

'Things don't sound quite as bad as I'd expected. Ever since you came to see me that day at the hospital I've been waiting for the creditors to close in.'

'Nothing like that's going to happen. You just take it easy. You're convalescing, remember, and that means a complete break from work. So listen, if you don't hear from me again, everything's fine. OK?'

'OK,' Imogen agreed.

'Take care, then.'

'Oh, Jim,' she said quickly, pausing a moment before asking, striving to keep indifference in her voice, 'have you heard from Dad lately?'

'Yeah,' he said, the conviviality of his tone a shade forced. 'I stopped round to see him on Sunday, told him you were out of hospital.'

'What did he say?'

There was a brief silence at the other end of the phone and then Jim said, his voice flatter, more honest,

'Look, you know you'll always be in the wrong where he's concerned. Why don't you just leave it?'

'Because I can't. Jim, I've got to know who my real father is. I've thought about it almost non-stop since I've been home. I don't like the thought of confronting Dad, but I can't live with my background a complete question mark. I've got to know what happened, why Mother didn't press for a divorce.'

There was a long, uneasy pause, then Jim said, 'I suppose I can understand that.'

'I hoped you would. I wanted your OK before I went ahead and spoke to Dad.'

'Then you've got it. Look after yourself. I'll be in touch.'

Imogen replaced the receiver. The news on the business front was better than she'd been expecting. She put her hand on the phone again.

Now that she had Jim's agreement there was no reason for her to delay contacting her father any longer. Before her resolve could falter she dialled his number. He'd shown little enough concern for her but, even so, she was sensitive about deliberately raising issues that had injured perhaps more than his pride. She stiffened a little as she heard him answer.

'Hello, Dad,' she began. 'It's me, Imogen.'

'Jim tells me you're back with Kirk.' Her father's voice was crisp and clearly modulated. Its customary lack of warmth seemed accentuated by the telephone.

'Yes,' she confirmed.

'I'm pleased to hear it,' he said, adding, so that it sounded like an afterthought, 'and to hear that you're out of hospital.'

'Dad, I want to talk to you. Could you come round? It's important.'

'Then let's talk about it now. I've got a very busy week ahead.'

'It's not something I can talk about on the phone.'

'You're making rather a mystery about this, aren't you?' he said, his tone faintly derisive. 'But all right, if it's important I'll look in for half an hour tomorrow morning. Expect me at ten.'

She didn't try to prolong the conversation. She said goodbye, already apprehensive about what she had started.

At breakfast the next morning she felt tense and on edge. She had not expected to see Kirk, he usually left the house earlier than this. Jeanne was upstairs making the beds. As she joined him in the kitchen he set aside the *Financial Times* he'd been reading.

In his steel-grey suit he looked urbane and disturbingly self-assured. His white shirt emphasised the tanned swarthiness of his skin. A tinge of colour crept into her face as she was reminded that she still found him attractive. She noted the firm line of his jaw. Against her will she remembered how in the early days of their marriage she had slid her fingers caressingly along his face, feeling the male roughness of it.

'So, what are your plans for today?' Kirk asked.

She poured herself a cup of coffee, avoiding his gaze as she deliberately didn't mention that her father was calling round.

'I may sit out in the garden later on. I want to

phone Jim first though, about the business.'

'You're not up to the strain of work yet.'

'A business doesn't run itself,' she said. 'You should know that.'

'No business would with that clown of a brother of yours at the helm,' he observed drily.

Apprehensive about confronting her father, she flared quickly into anger.

'Perhaps Jim doesn't have your ruthlessness,' she agreed, 'but I'd rather be in business with him than have any dealings of any kind with you.'

She saw his eyes harden and regretted her comment.

'One day,' he said, his voice clipped, 'when New Radiance has gone to the wall, I may remind you of that statement.'

He stood up and, picking up the paper, left the room. His words stayed menacingly in her mind. After Jim's phone call she had felt more optimistic about the business, but Kirk's prophecy frightened her a little. When it came to assessing a company's prospects his judgements were unerringly accurate.

Restlessly she took her coffee through into the lounge. She knew she wouldn't be able to settle to anything till after she had seen her father. As always, he was exactly on time. Jeanne answered the door to him and showed him in.

In his mid-fifties, he had an attractive, lined face with hard, contemptuous eyes, thick brows and dusty-blond hair. He was a robust man, solid without fat, and with a manner of brisk self-confidence.

'Now what's all this about, that you had to see me so urgently?' he began as he sat down in the armchair opposite her.

'That's how it always was even when I was growing up, wasn't it? I always needed a reason if we were going to talk.'

'I really haven't got time to sit here and talk

nonsense. I've got an appointment at eleven.'

Imogen took a steadying breath. This wasn't how she wanted to handle it, but he was giving her no choice.

'All right, then,' she conceded before saying, her voice perfectly steady, 'I want you to tell me about my father.'

A look of shocked anger came into his face. There was a sudden silence, dense with recriminations, then, covering his reaction, he said in a loud exasperated voice,

'What on earth are you talking about? Are you still suffering from concussion?'

'No, I know exactly what I'm saying. Till now I never could work out why you were always so distant with me, why everything I did was always wrong. I tried so hard to be the kind of daughter you wanted, but I wasn't in with a chance, was I? You've never forgiven me for not being yours.'

'Well, perhaps it's just as well you've found out, though God knows how you have. Now I don't even have to put up an act of being your father. I've condoned your mother's adultery for all these years and, what's more, brought up another man's child. Frankly, I've done enough. And as for being a disappointment, yes, you are. You're just like your mother. She couldn't be true to her marriage vows and you haven't been true to yours.'

'You must know that's unfair,' she said swiftly. 'You've always been ready to criticise me for no reason. Do you have any idea of how I've felt, knowing that you cared about Jim but that I never counted, and never knowing why?' She got up and put an impulsive hand on his arm. 'Dad, I love you. I know it must be hard, but can't you try to accept me? I want to find out about my real father, but you'll always be important to me.'

He stood up, brushing her hand aside.

'Your real father,' he repeated bitterly. 'So you want to know about him—then I'll tell you. He worked at the Austrian Embassy. Your mother had a cheap, tawdry affair with him, and then he left her.'

'I don't believe Mother would have been involved in anything like that,' Imogen protested with angry loyalty.

'Oh, so you'd rather not know. First you wanted to know about your father, but now you find out he was a cheap, no-good womaniser you don't like it.'

'I want to know his name.'

'There's no point. He's dead.'

'I don't believe you.'

'He was killed the year you were born.'

'So that's why Mother didn't leave you! It wasn't that my father deserted her.'

'Yes, you'd like to build up a romantic dream about him, wouldn't you?' he sneered. 'I wonder what your husband would think if he knew the truth. The only thing you ever did that I could be proud of was marry well, and now if you persist with this you'll wreck even that. Do you think Kirk's going to want the illegitimate daughter of a playboy for a wife? If you've got any sense you'll keep this as much of a secret as I've always done. I gave you as good an upbringing as any man could be expected to. You owe me at least the assurance that the past stays buried.'

'You needn't worry,' Imogen retorted. 'I've no intention of telling Kirk. He married me to be the rose in his buttonhole. I know exactly what he'd think of me if he knew.'

Her father looked at her and then, slightly pacified, said,

'Well, you do have a modicum of sense—I'll give you that. And we can go on as before. I'll still see you occasionally. When you're better, you and Kirk can come round for drinks one evening.

'No,' she said hollowly. 'I'm not coming just to keep up the façade for your friends. I don't mean anything to you at all, do I?'

'What would you expect?' he asked curtly. 'As far as I'm concerned, I only have one son. I never had a daughter.'

In the hall, the phone started ringing.

'I don't think there's any more to be said,' he told her brusquely as he moved towards the door. 'It's up to you whether you want to keep the façade going, as you call it.'

The ringing stopped and then Jeanne came in.

'Someone's phoning from your salon, Mrs Cameron.'

'OK, Jeanne,' Imogen said, her voice harassed. 'Dad . . . '

He cut across her.

'You're busy and so am I. I'll see myself out.'

She followed him into the hall, but he banged the front door behind him without looking back. She felt hollow and shaky, her father's words, 'I never had a daughter,' leaving her too numbed to feel the sharp rise of pain that would come later.

A shade abstractedly she picked up the receiver.

'Yes, what is it?'

'Imogen? It's Jackie. I'm sorry to trouble you at home.'

'Don't worry,' she said, forcing her attention to the demands of the business. 'What's the problem?'

'Well, I can't get hold of Jim and the wages haven't come through.'

'They haven't? I can't understand it. Look, don't worry, I'll get straight on to the bank and get it sorted out.'

'I'm sorry,' Jackie repeated, 'but you know how it

is at the end of the month. The girls rely on getting their wages.'

'I know. It's all right, Jackie. You were right to phone me.

Apprehension didn't hit her immediately. Jim had assured her that there would be money to meet the company's immediate outgoings. It was only as she waited to be put through to Mr Hollis that she began to feel a sudden premonition of calamity.

'Good morning, Mrs Cameron. How can I help you?'

'I'm phoning up to know why the wages haven't been paid into our employees' accounts as usual,' she began.

'Then it's obvious you haven't received my letter explaining that your company has reached the agreed overdraft limit. Without further collateral I'm afraid there can be no further advance.'

'But my brother came in to see you earlier in the week!' she protested in shocked incomprehension.

'When I explained the position to him,' Mr Hollis informed her. 'As soon as there's some money in the account, your employees' accounts will be credited.'

He rounded the conversation off smoothly. Imogen replaced the receiver slowly, almost as though it might shatter. She wasn't thinking immediately of Jim's irresponsible deception in letting her believe that they still had enough credit to pay their way. It was the company that was uppermost in her mind, *her* company, the business she had put so much of her energy into and which was now collapsing.

Suddenly she saw how much it meant to her. First, she had needed it as a way of proving her ability to her father. That reason had gone now, but her marriage was over. She was never going to find fulfilment in life from building a partnership with Kirk. The business was a means of justifying her existence. Its demands left no time for loneliness or regrets. It was just about all she had to give her life direction.

She thought back to what her father had told her. Her real father was dead—she had no reason to doubt that. It tied in too neatly with the fact that her mother hadn't pressed for a divorce. Would her natural father have loved her for what she was, freeing her from this pressing weight of the need to prove herself? Somehow she knew the answer. At the moment she didn't need to know any more about him than that and the fact that her mother had loved him.

The thought comforted her a little, making it easier to stave off the sense of defeat that lay like a cold snake round her heart. For an instant she imagined the inevitable compulsory winding up of the company, the freezing of its assets till the final auditing was done, the dismantling of the business that she had struggled so hard to launch and build up. And then non-acceptance suddenly reasserted itself. She wouldn't let this happen. As an employer she had a duty to see that her work-force was paid, and they would be, because she'd somehow pay them out of her own finances. She must go to the main salon, if only to restore confidence with the staff.

The doctor had warned her it was too early yet for her to drive because of her headaches and, in any case, Kirk had taken the Mercedes to work. The cab she rang for arrived just as Jeanne came into the hall from the kitchen.

'The taxi outside,' Jeanne began in concern. 'It's not for you?'

'Something's come up at work. I have to go out.'

'But you're supposed to be resting,' Jeanne protested anxiously. 'I promised Mr Cameron . . .'

'I shouldn't be long,' Imogen cut across her, putting a reassuring hand briefly on the girl's arm as she went past her.

It was only as Imogen got into the cab that she remembered that she should have slipped her tablets into her bag. She wouldn't stop to go back for them. Her mind was working frantically. The company had started to sink and she couldn't see a single way of saving it. If there was the least suspicion that New Radiance couldn't pay its way, the creditors would close in on her like hounds on wounded prey. At the back of her mind was her meeting with her father, but however hurt that had left her, there wasn't time to replay it in memory now.

The cab dropped her outside the shop and she went inside to a chorus of greetings from the staff. Jackie came towards her.

'Imogen!' she began with a smile. 'I never expected to see you this morning. Are you quite sure you're supposed to be back at work?'

'Quite sure.'

She paused to have a word individually with her staff and then she signalled to Jackie that she'd like to speak to her in her office. She walked through to the beauty salon area, noting as she did so that the jacuzzi was silent.

'I hope you didn't feel you had to come in just because I rang you,' Jackie began.

'It's time I looked in, anyway,' said Imogen, pressing her fingers against her left temple. 'About the wages—there's going to be a slight delay this month. Will you tell the girls they'll get their pay the middle of next week at the latest? I'm afraid with being in hospital I haven't caught up with seeing to the payroll.'

Jackie accepted the explanation. Obviously, she had no inkling that the company was so precariously balanced. She couldn't have, from the calmness with which she announced,

'While you're here, we've just had the estimate for fixing the jacuzzi. It's on your desk.'

'Thanks,' Imogen said a shade tautly, dismay hitting her with an effect not unlike the sensation induced by a lift dropping stone-like five storeys. 'I'll look at it.'

'Cup of coffee?' asked Jackie as she went out.

'No, thanks,' she said, marvelling that her voice could sound so even. 'Not just now.'

The door closed behind Jackie and Imogen quickly leafed through the papers for the estimate. Her vision seemed to be blurred and she blinked hard to clear it. This was the final unlooked-for expense, the final calamity. She put the papers down as a sickening, off-balance sensation surged over her. An all-pervading weakness was dragging her into darkness. The head-ache that had been with her mildly since her father had called thudded into slashing pain. She made a faint effort to get up, to call to Jackie, before blackness enveloped her and she collapsed unconscious over the desk.

CHAPTER SEVEN

IMOGEN came round to find she was lying on the sofa in her office. She was frighteningly weak, so limp that she seemed to have no strength at all. Kirk was standing over her, his dark eyes searching her face. Bewildered, she could not immediately work out how he came to be with her.

'I must have fainted,' she began unsteadily.

'Just what are you trying to do?' he asked tersely. 'Get back into hospital?'

'I only fainted,' she said, with more courage than she felt. 'There's no need to make a big thing out of it. You needn't worry, I'll be able to play the part of hostess when the Ellands arrive.'

She slid her legs off the sofa and then gave a slight cry as dizziness swept her again. Kirk sat beside her, drawing her close, and helplessly she turned her head against his shoulder until the sickening giddiness subsided a little. His fingers were biting into her skin and, dazed as she was, she could sense the anger he was holding so closely in check.

'My car's outside on the forecourt. Do you feel strong enough to walk to it?'

'I haven't finished here yet,' she protested, pulling away from him, and dropping her head in her hands.

'You're absolutely finished here,' he said savagely. He went over to her desk and snatched up the estimate that she had been looking at before she collapsed. 'This joke outfit you call a company has finally fallen apart, hasn't it? That's why you're here.'

'Stop it!' she said faintly her face taut and pinched.

He came back to her, taking her by the shoulders, forcing her to face him as he demanded,

'Why didn't you tell me you'd reached your credit limit?'

'Tell *you?*' she repeated contemptuously.

Kirk stared at her for a long moment, his eyes cold and bitter, his grip tightening with a bruising force he seemed not to care about.

'Enough said,' he commented, his voice as hard and remote as his eyes.

'So now I'm financially dependent on you as well,' she said. 'That must give you a great deal of satisfaction.'

'Yes,' he agreed brutally. 'You *are* financially dependent on me, and from now on you can start acting like my wife.'

'What do you mean?' asked Imogen in an apprehensive rush.

He pulled her to her feet.

'We'll sort out what I mean later.'

There was a tap at the door and Jackie came in with a glass of brandy.

'It's all right, Jackie,' Kirk said. 'I'm taking my wife home now.'

Jackie nodded.

'I hope you soon feel better, Imogen.'

Imogen gave her a faltering smile. She couldn't trust her voice.

Kirk escorted her out of the shop and held the car door for her as she got in. As he pulled out on to the main road she said dully,

'I suppose Jackie phoned you to say I'd fainted.'

'No, Jeanne phoned me. Luckily, she had the sense to get straight on to me as soon as you left the house.'

'How nice!' Imogen exclaimed tautly. 'Why, this is as good as having me under house arrest!'

'Don't push me, Imogen,' he said, flickering a hard,

hot glance as her. 'You've taxed my patience enough of late.'

She turned her head away and then after a moment's silence she said in a low voice,

'It would have been easier all round if I hadn't come out of that car crash.'

He pulled the car to the side of the road and switched off, turning her savagely to face him.'

'Don't ever say that!' he told her furiously.

For an instant he held her rigid and then he released her. She shrank away from him, then, suddenly and without warning, her strained nerves broke abruptly and she began to cry. Wordlessly Kirk started the car again while Imogen sat beside him, uselessly trying to suppress tears. She despised herself for showing this weakness in front of him, but her whole life was in ruins. She couldn't keep up a pretence of courage any longer. The company was going under, her father had finished with her completely and Kirk had defeated her in every way.

They arrived back at the house. Kirk took her arm as she got out of the car. She had stopped crying but she looked pale and shaken.

Jeanne came to the door.

'I hope you didn't mind my phoning your husband,' she began, a shade anxiously.

'I'm quite sure you had your instructions.'

Jeanne looked at her a mite incomprehendingly, as though uncertain as to her meaning.

'You'd better get some rest,' said Kirk, interrupting the exchange. 'I'll phone the doctor and then I want to talk to you.'

'There's no need to trouble the doctor.' She trailed off as she saw his expression. 'All right,' she agreed miserably.

She was just getting into bed when Kirk joined her. He came into her room as of right and stood at the foot of the bed, studying her with slightly narrowed eyes.

'I take it you want to save the business,' he began.

'It's too late now, isn't it?' she said flatly.

'I don't know,' he said. 'It's up to you.'

'What do you mean?'

'I mean I'm prepared to put seven thousand into it as of now, plus give a personal guarantee to the bank for a further five.'

Imogen glanced at him in disbelief.

'But why would you do that?'

He sat down on the bed. The easy relaxation of his body was that of a man totally in command of the situation. She was conscious of the latent strength of his male build and of her own powerlessness. She had never felt this way with Graeme. Their relationship had been sane, warm, comfortable. It was only with Kirk that she felt this shattering edge of unease, this awareness of her sexuality that meant, when she was with him, being a woman held a new, vibrant meaning for her.

'For the reasons I gave you before when you turned the loan down,' he said. 'But that aside, I've always felt that with the right financial direction, New Radiance was a very viable proposition. There are some tidy profits to be picked up from salvage operations.'

'And how are you going to ensure that the business has the right financial direction?' she asked suspiciously.

It was hard to fence with him when she felt so drained, when defeat lay like a pall on her spirits and when he held all the aces.

'For as long as my money's keeping the company afloat, I have a say in its running.'

'Jim will never agree to that.'

'I think he will. He hasn't much choice. Neither, for that matter, have you.'

Imogen looked at him uncertainly. The business was enormously important to her. Jim might have wrecked the company's financial stability, but the salons had a reputation for high standards and faultless customer service. With more backing, she knew she could eventually make New Radiance successful. She was certain she could. She had to. It was the only thing she had left. Kirk might rate Lydia more highly than her in bed, but if she could once make New Radiance pay again, at least he'd have to respect her business sense.

'I don't want the company to fold,' she said.

'Is that an agreement?' he asked, before adding swiftly, 'Perhaps I ought to spell out the rest of the terms just so that you know exactly what you're committing yourself to.'

She remembered what he had said to her at the salon, that she was his wife and that he intended her to be just that.

'I don't come as part of the deal,' she said, knowing that she sounded a shade breathless, and angry with herself for betraying her apprehension.

She was a woman, not a flustered girl. She ought to be able to rebuff his demands with more assurance than this. He put his hand on her wrist and traced his fingers up along her arm with, it seemed to her, the deliberate slowness of conscious power.

A blinding knife of pain tore through her head and instinctively she caught hold of his hand, turning to him instead of away from him, her fingers tightening under his firm grip. She opened her eyes as the agony subsided, to find he was watching her, his face haggard with what looked like tightly controlled anger. She slid her hand out of his and repeated,

'I don't come as part of the deal.'

'I thought I'd made it clear I didn't want you under duress,' he said, his voice clipped. 'You seem rather slow to accept the fact. If I'd intended forcing you to sleep with me you wouldn't be sleeping alone in this room now.'

'Then, if I misunderstood you,' she said, colouring slightly, 'what did you mean by other terms?'

He deliberately let his gaze travel to her throat and the creamy curve of her shoulders.

'The terms have nothing to do with the fact that you're my wife. I've never believed in mixing business with pleasure.'

'Really?' she said with deliberate scepticism. His relaxed, sensual voice unsettled her. 'And Lydia,' she continued, 'just how do you categorise her, business associate or mistress?'

'That's rather an old-fashioned term to use, isn't it? You're hardly in the position to play the injured wife, Imogen, or had you forgotten you'd told me that you and Peter were lovers?'

She didn't answer. There was a short silence, then he asked, his voice unhurried,

'Does it bother you, my relationship with Lydia?'

'No,' she lied, hoping her tone wasn't too sharp to be convincing.

She supposed it was because she was weak and shaken but, suddenly, the thought of him touching Lydia as he had touched her was insupportable. Her heart contracted with something deeper than jealousy or wounded pride. She mustn't think of it, mustn't imagine them together. When she was calmer it wouldn't bother her so much.

'You still haven't told me the terms,' she reminded him.

'That for the next three weeks you turn everything you've been handling with the running of the company over to me. You don't seem to realise that you're ill and that you've got to have complete rest. A convalescent wife isn't going to make a very good hostess.

I don't want you going anywhere near the salons until you're fit.'

'But I'll have to know what's happening,' she protested.

'No. You're just going to have to trust me.'

There was a long uneasy pause and then she agreed reluctantly,

'All right. After all, as you've said, what option do I have?'

The doorbell rang.

'That'll be Dr Mortimer,' said Kirk, as though, she thought, nothing of any real importance had taken place between them.

There was certainly no shading of triumph in his voice. It surprised her, for most certainly he had gained another victory over her. He'd said the company would collapse and it had.

He went out and she heard his firm, lithe tread on the stairs.

It was some while later when Dr Mortimer came into her room. In his early fifties, he had an efficient, pleasant manner.

'I understand you had a fainting spell this morning,' he began.

He couldn't know the strain she was under. As much as the devastation of learning the company had exceeded its credit limit was the shock of rejection from her father.

She nodded, and he said, as he bent closer to examine her eyes. 'You've been having a lot of head-aches following your accident?'

'Yes.'

'Do the tablets you're on control the pain?'

'Pretty well.'

'Mm,' he said as he sat back. 'How are you sleeping?'

Imogen hesitated, wondering if she should tell him

that her sleep was disturbed by unusually vivid night-mares.

'Not quite as well as usual?' he queried.

'No,' she agreed. 'In fact, last night I scarcely slept at all.

'I'll give you some sleeping tablets.' He took his prescription pad out of his bag and continued talking as he wrote. 'I'll give you twenty just to get your normal pattern of sleep restored.'

He tore the prescription off the pad and placed it on the bedside table.

'It's really just a question of time,' he told her as he turned back to her. 'With complete rest, you'll be surprised how quickly you pick up.' He paused and then said, 'Anything you want to ask me?'

'Yes. How soon will it be before I can drive?'

'Certainly not till the headaches have cleared, and they may linger for a while yet. But apart from that restriction, so long as you make sure you get plenty of rest, you can carry on pretty much as normal. Tackle what you feel able to, but don't get over-tired.'

Imogen nodded.

'And of course,' he continued, 'there's no reason why you shouldn't resume normal marital relations, if you haven't already. In fact, you'll probably find it eases the build-up of tension that aggravates the head-aches.'

His medical frankness left her, for an imperceptible moment, at a loss.

'Thank you, doctor,' she managed evenly.

After all, if Kirk and she really had the close relationship that marriage implied, his remarks wouldn't have shocked her.

It was only when he had gone that she wondered if Kirk had mentioned the matter to him. The thought of it made her colour with resentment. How dared he! As if her refusal to sleep with him had anything to do with her state of health. The only reason he wanted her was because she was a challenge and he felt he had a right to her.

She heard the front door close as the doctor left and then Kirk came upstairs to her.

'I'll get your prescription made up on my way to the office,' he said as he went purposefully over to the bedside table.

'Just what did you say to Dr Mortimer?' she asked accusingly.

'I filled him in with the details of the accident. Why?'

'And seemingly about our sex life.'

He gave her a puzzled glance and she realised she'd been mistaken.

'It doesn't matter,' she said quickly.

'No, I'm intrigued,' said Kirk, sitting on the bed beside her. 'Tell me more.'

She maintained a determined silence for an instant, then said, meeting his challenging eyes with a touch of defiance,

'He said there was no physical reason for us not to resume marital relations. I think that was how he expressed it.'

'Had that been worrying you?' Kirk asked with unusual gentleness. 'That physically . . . that I might hurt you?'

'No,' she said quickly, conscious that the tone of his voice was sending a strange flicker of warmth through her. 'It hadn't crossed my mind.' She broke off and added matter-of-factly, with an abrupt change of topic, 'The prescription's for sleeping tablets.'

Kirk gave a brief smile that held little amusement.

'Trouble sleeping?' he asked. 'I don't seem to remember you having that problem before when we were together.'

She knew what he meant. His lovemaking had

drawn her to such an ever-greater maturity of response that the complete physical and emotional catharsis made sleep come easily afterwards.

'The tablets will do the trick,' she said coolly.

'Are you sure?' he asked tauntingly. 'When you're used to sharing a bed it's not easy to sleep alone.'

'I'm not used to sharing a bed,' she informed him.

She saw the questioning lift of his eyebrows and amended what she had said by adding quickly,

'Peter and I weren't living together. He didn't spend all his nights with me.'

'You must miss him,' Kirk said brutally. 'Oh, I know the impression you give to other men, a shade distant despite the friendliness, that very slight coolness that conveys unavailability. But that's not the case, is it? You can be quite the temptress when you want to be, and you're woman enough to need a man. You might have protested that morning when you woke up to find you'd slept alongside me, but you'd have let me take you easily enough the night before.'

'Leave me alone! I don't want to talk about this.'

He put his hand under her chin, forcing her to meet his gaze.

'Why not? Or are you afraid to face the truth?'

She didn't answer and he said softly,

'You'll come to me in the end.'

She turned away from him in stony anger and he stood up.

Imogen waited till he had reached the door, then she said in a reluctant rush, her voice cold,

'Kirk, my staff haven't been paid their wages.'

'Right, I'll see to it.'

Emotionally exhausted, Imogen slept well into the afternoon, when she tried, without success, to contact Jim. She started to be worried about him. Where could he have got to? It was with quite a feeling of relief that she looked out of her bedroom window to see his car turning into the drive. Jeanne answered the door to him as Imogen came downstairs.

He looked tense, his usual cheerfulness replaced by a nervous energy. He waited till they were in the lounge and Jeanne was out of earshot before saying,

'You haven't really agreed to accept this loan from Kirk, have you?'

'Financially, it's a good offer.'

'It's no offer at all if it gives him the right to interfere in the company's running.'

'Without his money we won't have a company any more,' she pointed out, before asking, 'Jim, why ever didn't you tell me the bank had refused to extend our credit limit?'

Jim put his hands in his pockets and strolled over to the window.

'Because I didn't want to worry you. I hoped I'd be able to raise the cash some other way.' He swung back to her as he continued abruptly, 'I'm not agreeing to this. I'm getting out. As of now, I'm resigning from the company.'

'Jim, don't be so ridiculous! You haven't got another job.'

There was a short silence, then he said harshly,

'All right, then. I'll carry on for a while at least, but you'd better tell that husband of yours that I have an equal say in the running of the company. And, what's more, I'm not having him scrutinising the accounts.'

'Be reasonable. He has every right to. You're over-reacting.'

'*You* can say that,' Jim cut across her with unusual vehemence, 'because you don't have to work with him.'

'No,' she agreed bitterly. 'I have to live with him.'

'If you're not happy, walk out. You've done it before.'

Jeanne appeared in the doorway and asked,

'Would you like me to make a pot of tea?'

'No!' Jim roared at her.

'Jim, really!' Imogen exclaimed as, startled, Jeanne quickly withdrew. She could never remember seeing her brother this harassed before.

'Listen,' she continued more calmly, 'I'm not any happier about the set-up than you are, but I've worked too hard to lose everything now, and frankly, it's a pretty fair offer of Kirk's.'

Jim looked at her as if tempted to say more, then, with a low exclamation of futility, he strode out of the room.

'Jim!' she called after him, going to follow him.

She reached the hall as the front door slammed to behind him. For a minute she stood there in troubled incomprehension. She'd known roughly how he'd react, but she had never expected him to be so irrationally vehement.

Jeanne was out that evening at an English class. It was the first time Imogen had been alone in the house with Kirk since coming home, and it made her feel slightly insecure. Somehow she could not forget the doctor's matter-of-fact statement that physical closeness with her husband might be beneficial in releasing the build-up of tension. He couldn't know that much of the strain she was under was caused by being under the same roof as Kirk again.

She changed into a pale green dress that suited her fragile colouring. It was the first time in some while that she had noticed how she looked. She stepped into her high-heeled court shoes and glanced again in the full-length mirror. Kirk's words spoke to her out of memory. 'I know the impression you give to men, a shade distant despite the friendliness . . . ' She turned away quickly, before she could remember the rest of his comments or link them with the ones her father had made about her.

She went downstairs to put the finishing touches to the salad that Jeanne had helped her prepare. She was in the kitchen when Kirk came in from work. He kissed her cursorily on the cheek, but even so, the gesture disturbed her. It also annoyed her. When only this afternoon he'd carelessly mentioned his mistress to her, a token kiss of affection was utterly meaningless.

'Jim called here this afternoon,' she said, her voice level, a shade cool.

'He's none too happy with the business arrangement,' Kirk commented.

'Well, he's agreed to it at any rate.'

'Which suggests he has marginally more sense than I gave him credit for,' he said drily.

Imogen hoped the evening would be tranquil. She'd had enough strain for one day. She succeeded in keeping the conversation innocuous over dinner. As they went through into the lounge she had a sudden wish that it could always be like this between them, that there were no hidden resentments, no reasons for hostility.

'Jeanne mentioned that your father called round this morning,' said Kirk, as he sat down in the armchair opposite her. 'You didn't say. Have you finally patched things up with him?'

She looked away, her eyes darkening a little.

'I don't think I'm ever going to do that. I'm just not the daughter he wanted.'

'I can't think why.'

There was an irony in his comment that made her suddenly unable to answer for fear her voice would betray her. Kirk stood up and joined her on the sofa, putting a hand under her chin as his dark eyes probed hers.

'What's wrong?' he asked, his tone gentle. 'You're very close to tears. It's not the business, is it? Because you don't have to worry about that any more.'

'It's just that I'm tired,' she said, her voice constrained. 'It's been a rough day. I think I'll have an early night.'

Her emotions were dangerously out of control. His gentleness was destroying her defences against him. It was at times like this when she could easily be betrayed into thinking that their marriage wasn't smashed irredeemably, that there was a bridge back across the gulf of misunderstandings. That was an illusion. If Kirk knew the truth about her, he'd see her as worthless.

She felt tension tightening her shoulders again as she fought against the increasing vibrations of pairing between them. There was a kind of lethal quality in the relaxed way he released her as though, she thought, he need not take one more step than was necessary because, as he'd predicted, she would come to him in the end.

'I've got your sleeping tablets,' he said, taking the small container from his jacket pocket.

'I don't think I'll need them tonight.'

'Are you sure? You seem rather tense.'

'It's been a very stressful day,' she reminded him a shade curtly.

The treacherousness of a moment ago had gone. She felt more sure of herself now that she seemed to have revived a flicker of the usual enmity between them.

'Do you want me to rub your shoulders for you?' Kirk asked.

'No,' she said, with a shade more emphasis than was necessary, getting swiftly to her feet.

'You're not afraid of me touching you, are you?' he said mockingly as he stood up, before perching on the arm of the sofa.

'Of course not,' she denied quickly.

'Then don't pull away.'

He drew her down beside him on the cushions. She knew that her breathing was coming more rapidly and hoped he wouldn't notice. She closed her eyes grimly as she felt his fingers drift against the taut muscles of her neck, fighting against the fierce pleasure of his touch.

'Relax,' he said. 'You've nothing to worry about now. There's money in New Radiance's account and your stylists will get their pay cheques tomorrow.'

'Well, that's something,' she acknowledged, knowing that whatever his motives she had reason to be grateful to him.

She was slightly ashamed that when he'd baled her out she'd not even offered the most cursory thanks in return. He'd shown over the Transit International contract he could be hard to the point of ruthlessness, but he'd been more generous than he need have over this. Repenting, she reached up and touched his hand with tentative fingers in a gesture that held more than a suggestion of tenderness. For an instant there was a silence, so acute it seemed timeless, then she said with some difficulty, 'If I haven't seemed appreciative of your loan, it's because I don't find it easy to accept charity.'

She felt his hand stiffen on her shoulder.

'I told you,' he said, his voice a shade clipped, 'it's an investment. I'm not a particularly charitable man when it comes to business dealings.'

Imogen didn't contradict him. His hands slipped round to undo the front buttons of her dress so he could massage her shoulders without the cloth coming between his firm, insistent fingers and her skin. She caught her breath and he remarked, his voice lazily amused,

'You start as if a man had never touched you before!'

'You have to admit this is a rather bizarre situation,' she said, keeping her voice cool and steady but only with an effort.

She felt his hands sliding over her bare shoulders, easing the tension from them with their expert touch. It was only the cessation of strain, she told herself resolutely, that made this treacherous warmth echo through her. She must keep a strict rein on her thoughts and not let her senses be seduced by his closeness and his deft capable hands that, despite everything, could still arouse her.

'You're fighting me,' he said perceptively. 'Come on, relax, let go.'

With a slight moan, Imogen closed her eyes and acquiesced. Her heart was thudding, the core of her being melting into compliance. Instinctively, she moved sensuously against him, her head tilted back against his shoulder as her eyes, smoky and inviting, met his.

'Imogen?' Her name was no more than a questioning murmur, then he drew her possessively towards him, his mouth coming down on hers.

She knew she should resist, but a crazy recklessness was sweeping her. What did it matter if there was no love between them, when he could kiss her with such demanding relentlessness, when he could make her drown in a vast sea of sensual delight? What did Lydia matter? She had to respond to him, to kiss him back with an urgency that matched his own, to press her body enticingly to his. His lips travelled to her throat. She felt the weight of his body on hers and realised he had eased her down on the sofa. Her fingers slid imploringly over his back, beneath his jacket, wanting a still deeper possession from him.

Neither of them heard the telephone for the first few minutes. And then its insistent ring brought

Imogen back to reality, and helplessly she pushed away from him, her senses still reeling from the havoc he had wrought. His arms loosened and she sat up, unable to meet his eyes, the telephone still shrilling. He caught hold of her arm, but the spell of a moment ago had broken and he saw only dismay and confusion in her face.

'Damn it, and damn you!' he grated savagely as he stood up and went to answer the phone.

Hurriedly she left the room, almost stumbling on the stairs in her haste to escape him. The bedroom door didn't have a lock. If only it had. Could she really blame him if he followed her, demanded she put out the fire that she had started? What on earth was wrong with her that, even knowing he had a mistress, she could act so wantonly with him?

She leaned for a moment against the closed door, her breathing coming in short gasps. She trembled a little as she remembered the feelings he had aroused in her. He had said she shivered as if no man had ever touched her before. Well, no man ever had, not the way he did.

This couldn't go on. She couldn't go on living with him with this unspent passion between them. Wearily she moved towards the bed and sank down on the floor beside it, resting her head against the mattress. Why didn't she just give in to him? she wondered. He was right: she did need the fulfilment only he could give her. Why had he made her discover these violent feelings within herself that made self-respect and independence meaningless beside the driving need for completeness with him? Maybe if she slept with him the passion would burn itself out.

CHAPTER EIGHT

THAT night, Imogen dreamed again the disturbed, confused nightmare about the car crash. Again she was running from the house, desperate to get away, knowing she had lost Kirk to Lydia for good and that the future was empty and desolate, for he would never share any part of it with her now. She woke up shivering, the bedclothes in a disordered tangle.

She snapped the light on. The silence of the night was dense. She looked at the clock. It was two-twenty, a dismal hour.

Pulling her wrap round her shoulders, she got out of bed. She wouldn't sleep now. It wasn't only that the fear and heartbreak of the nightmare took time to recede from her senses; it was also that it forced her to evaluate her feelings for Kirk.

She sat down in the armchair, tucking her feet up and huddling against the cushions. The night wasn't chilly, but she felt cold. She refused to think of the comfort of Kirk's arms that first evening home after she had woken, startled, from the enveloping horror of the nightmare. The sudden, unfettered physical attraction that had leapt into flaring prominence between them tonight had shocked her, making her despise herself. She tensed a little as she remembered the wanton recklessness that had swamped her. She had tried to hide from her feelings for him, rationalise them with a determined ingenuity, but she couldn't deny any longer that she wanted physical closeness with him, despite the fact that he didn't love her, despite Lydia. Why ever had she agreed to come back to him? It was only making her realise truths she didn't want to discover.

She slept fitfully just before the dawn came, to wake again at a little before seven. She looked pale, and not even the artfully applied eye-shadow and blusher quite disguised her wanness.

Jeanne was not yet up. Imogen didn't feel like breakfast, but she made a pot of tea. She was sitting at the kitchen table when Kirk joined her. The memory of the previous night lay dangerously between them. He studied her a moment, then said evenly as he sat down opposite her,

'Good morning. You're up very early.'

There was a short, brittle silence and then, pushing her chair back, she stood up and said in a low intense voice,

'I can't go on like this. It was crazy of me to think that we could live together again. I won't stay here and be your bed partner just because I happen to be available and we're still legally married.' Her eyes, dark and stormy, met his. 'You may be able to look on sex as a purely physical need, but for me, it's got to mean something more, and living here and being kept by you I'm starting to feel like some sort of geisha girl. I feel cheap.'

Kirk didn't answer immediately. His face was unreadable and his voice when he spoke had an austere calmness to it.

'Sit down,' he said.

A shade reluctantly, Imogen did as he asked.

'I had no idea,' he began, his voice clipped and a mite sardonic, 'that I made you feel cheap. Obviously I don't treat you with the reverence Graeme did in your perfect, pure relationship.'

She looked away.

'I don't want to talk about this.'

'Well, I do,' he cut across her, before going on with

all the keen-witted provocation of a lawyer for the prosecution, 'I can't quite fathom why you slept with Peter. Just how did you square that with your high-minded notions that you still belong to Graeme?'

'I don't belong to anyone, not even to you, and I don't owe you an explanation for anything.'

'You *are* still legally bound to me by marriage,' he reminded her, 'but you needn't worry, I won't make any physical demands on you again. Yours isn't the only bed. There are others warmer and more exciting than yours.'

His parallel with what Lydia had implied about her sexuality hit at her self-esteem as a woman. So he *had* found she lacked the sexual charisma it took to satisfy him. Once the seduction was over, his interest in her waned. She couldn't provide him with a physical relationship that was enhancing and powerful enough to hold him.

'Then I'll pack my things,' she said quietly, lifting her chin as she met his eyes so he wouldn't see how his words stung.

'You will not.'

'What do you mean?' she asked angrily. 'I'm tired of this charade you call a marriage, and I'd have thought you would be, too.'

'If you remember, the agreement was that you act the part of my wife till the Transit International contract is secure. And in any case, you're not well enough to be on your own.'

His dismissive, impersonal concern made a lonely sense of insignificance tighten around her heart. She would have rather he felt anything for her so long as it wasn't this fog of indifference there was no way of penetrating.

'I don't see how you can expect me to go on living here,' she said shortly.

'Because, strange as it may seem,' he said harshly,

'the contract aside, I find I do still care about what happens to you. In fact, I feel sorry for you.'

'Well, you needn't, because I don't want your pity!'

'There's something rather pitiable about you altogether. Your venture into the business world hasn't been a success. You can't make a lasting relationship with a man because emotionally you're still tied to a ghost.'

'Don't you sit in judgement on me,' she said furiously, cutting across him, 'and don't class New Radiance as a failure, because I'm not through with it yet.'

'Then I'll await the developments with interest,' he said with a light edge of sarcasm.

'You really rate my abilities as zero, don't you?' she said bitterly. 'I'm only surprised you ever wanted to marry me in the first place. No wonder my father thinks so highly of you. The two of you have a lot in common. You're both money and power obsessed, and you both share the view that I'm completely incompetent.'

'If you *were* completely incompetent,' said Kirk, his words clipped, 'I'd have washed my hands of you long before this.'

'And just where has all your success got you?' she said, retaliating all the more vengefully because she had once loved him, and maybe still did, however vehemently she denied it. 'You've got a hollow shell of a marriage and a wife who's come to hate you. Perhaps Graeme did mean I couldn't get a relationship going with you, but at least with him I knew what love meant. He was more of a man than you are, even if he didn't have your money and influence.'

Kirk took a menacing step nearer, his eyes dark and angry, and she should have known she'd gone too far. But instead, she felt only a mollifying sense of redress that she had at last succeeded in evening the score a little.

'Was he?' he said savagely as he took hold of her by the shoulders, swinging her to face him, his hands gripping her with brutal force.

'Let go of me!' she demanded, striving to keep apprehension from showing in her voice.

'Well, for all he was such a man, he never had you, did he?' he snapped furiously.

'Stop it,' she said swiftly, her voice a frightened gasp as he pulled her close, pinioning her to him.

She tried to turn her head away, but before she could, he pushed her chin back with angry fingers and kissed her forcefully, his mouth hard and cruel on hers. For all the urgency of their lovemaking, he had never before touched her sexually with anything but gentleness, and the violence she sensed in him now frightened her. She struggled against him in a frenzy of alarm, her blouse tearing as she pulled away.

She staggered backwards, her eyes wide with fear, steadying herself against the work top that made further retreat impossible. Kirk came closer, jerking her towards him.

'It's too late to be acting the affronted virgin,' he said roughly, 'or had you forgotten you'd told me you and Peter were lovers? I've respected your feelings for your dead fiancé long enough!'

He combed his fingers into her hair, his mouth determined and relentless on hers as he kissed her again. She pushed ineffectually against him, as he arched her body backwards. The memory of the times when he had swept her with him in a tumult of helpless desire made her fear of what was happening now and her rebellion against it all the more intense.

His grip slackened a little. She scarcely registered it as, wrenching herself free and too shaken to see how haggard he looked, she slapped him across the face with all the force she had. He took the blow with an emptiness of expression that signalled the flashpoint of tension between them was past. Nerved for his anger, the sudden cessation of emotional stress was too much and she sat down weakly, putting her elbows on the kitchen table and covering her face with her hands.

She flinched as he caught hold of her arm. Looking up at him she began in a defensive rush,

'Peter's not my lover. He's never been my lover.'

For an instant Kirk kept his vice-like grip on her, his eyes dark and hot, and then, recognising honesty, he released her.

'You mean you've never slept with him?' he asked, his voice curiously flat.

Imogen forced herself to meet his gaze, drawing her blouse across her bare shoulder with fingers that were not quite steady as she spoke.

'No, I've never slept with Peter. I've never slept with anyone but you. Does that satisfy you?'

'Then why the hell did you tell me that you had?' he asked in a voice suddenly vibrant with passion.

'Because I wanted to hurt you. I didn't think your pride could take the thought that you'd lost one of your acquisitions,' she said before sweeping on bitterly, 'But now you know the truth, so your pride's safe. I was a virgin when I married you, and no one but you has ever touched me. It's ironic, isn't it, when I hate you so, that that should be the case?'

'Imogen . . .'

'Don't come near me. Don't you ever come near me or touch me again,' she said, getting swiftly to her feet and running quickly upstairs.

She could feel a headache coming on and she went straight over to her dressing-table for her tablets. She was trembling from reaction. For a few terrifying moments in the kitchen when Kirk had kissed her so savagely she had felt a sudden fear he was going to take her by force. She had never before seen the violence of emotion he kept so closely in check. The thought of what might so nearly have happened, what could still happen, left her shocked and drained.

Her blouse, she saw, was too badly torn to be mended. She took it off, seeing in the mirror the red marks on her shoulders where Kirk had caught hold of her so roughly. Water would soothe them. She unzipped her skirt and went into the en-suite bathroom, where she finished undressing. The stream of water over her body from the shower calmed her, making her more rational.

Just how had she expected Kirk to behave, she thought wearily, when she had taunted him over Graeme? Rights of possession were important to him. She should have known better than to provoke him so deliberately. But she wouldn't be so rash again. She was leaving. This morning had warned her of the danger of carrying on with an outward pretence of marriage.

Above the noise of the water she didn't immediately hear the knock at the door. She glanced round with wary eyes, turning the taps off quickly and pulling her towelling robe on over her wet body. She was tying the sash with agitated fingers as Kirk came into the room.

'What do you want?' she asked with distrustful hostility.

'To apologise,' he said. 'I shouldn't have been so rough with you.'

She came slowly into the bedroom but kept well away from him, making sure that the bed stayed as a barrier between them.

'Well?' she asked. 'Don't you want to comment on my relationship with Peter? You've always found plenty to remark on the fact that Graeme and I never slept together.'

'No, I don't want to comment.'

She stared at him coldly without speaking, pushing up the rather long sleeves of her robe.

'I see I bruised your wrist,' he observed.

'I thought perhaps you intended raping me,' she said curtly, forcing her voice to strength.

She saw the look of surprise that crossed his face before he said sarcastically,

'You really do have a high opinion of me, don't you? I don't need satisfaction from you that badly.'

Imogen didn't answer and he gave her a sharp, probing glance before saying, more gently,

'If I frightened you, and I obviously did, then I'm sorry.'

She nodded, accepting his apology and the assurance that he had never intended forcing her to have sex with him. She supposed she had always trusted him. For a moment that trust had flickered. Now it was back, and she realised what it meant to her.

There was a short pause, then she said,

'I'll be here for when the Ellands arrive, but till then I think it's best I move out.'

'Why?'

She looked disbelievingly at him.

'Why? You ask that after the row we've just had?'

'I'd say it's cleared the air,' said Kirk before observing with a touch of amusement, 'Do you know you're dripping water all over the carpet?'

'You didn't give me much time to get dry,' she reminded him.

'True,' he acknowledged, stepping forward to pick up her blouse that lay discarded on the bed. 'I'm sorry about your blouse. I'll buy you another.'

'You don't have to.'

'Has it never occurred to you I might like buying you things?'

Her eyes went to his in surprise, a sudden pleasure at his words sweeping through her. He came towards her, stopping as he drew near, before, when she didn't take a step back, placing his hands on her shoulders and kissing her cheek. She didn't resist him. Instead she went into his arms, pressing her face against his substantial shoulder. His arms tightened round her, and for an instant it seemed as if their communication went deeper than words ever could. Then, recovering herself, she disengaged from his embrace and took a step back. It was the first time since she had come back to him that they had used touch as a way of making up.

The next couple of weeks were calmer. Kirk worked late, and when he did come home he spent much of the evening in the study. Mostly their conversation consisted of his enquiries as to her health and her conventional replies. He treated her as he might a visitor to the house, making no encroachments on her.

Yet things were different between them. The argument that had flared so rapidly into violence that morning in the kitchen had forced Imogen into saying things to him she'd meant to keep suppressed. She didn't show her feelings easily. Kirk was somehow changing that.

But, despite the assurances she gave him, she felt far from well. She didn't tell him how often the headaches recurred, or that lack of sleep made her listless during the day. When she went back to Dr Mortimer, she deliberately didn't tell Kirk of her appointment.

The cab dropped her off home after her visit to the surgery and she noted uneasily that Kirk's Mercedes was in the drive. She let herself in and went through into the lounge. Kirk joined her.

'I've just stopped home because I need your signature on a couple of cheques,' he began as he sat down on the sofa beside her and handed her the company cheque-book and a pen.

She glanced at the amounts and the drawers, seeing that the cheques were to New Radiance's hair-care and beauty suppliers. She signed quickly and as she passed the cheque book back to him, said impulsively,

'I want to start work again.'

'No,' he said firmly. 'Business is hassle. Jim and I don't see eye to eye on anything, and I don't want you involved in any heated family arguments, not until you're up to it.'

'Just the same,' she said, 'I've been away long enough. I can't go on sitting at home, waiting for these awful headaches to finally clear. If I was at work it might take my mind off them. I've been told to rest and then they'll stop, but I have rested and they don't.'

'But you told me the headaches weren't troubling you any more,' Kirk said questioningly.

'They're not bad enough to keep me from working,' she lied. 'I suppose they are easier than they have been.'

He let her stammer on until she faltered, knowing that he didn't believe her.

He replaced the pen she had handed him in his inside jacket pocket and asked astutely,

'Were you at the doctor's this morning?'

The pause before she replied was answer enough.

'Then I think that settles the question of your starting work again,' he said decidedly. 'But when you do, there are going to be some changes.'

'What sort of changes?' she asked.

'For one thing, the management structure has got

to alter. It's time you started taking more responsibility for the financing of the company. I imagine it's all Jim can do to keep his personal bank account out of the red without being allowed free rein with the company cheque-book.'

'Jim handles the financial side of the company quite ably,' she said. 'He doesn't like interference.'

'No, I can well imagine.'

'What are you trying to imply?'

'I'm not implying anything,' he said, his words very distinct. 'I'm spelling it out in capital letters. Jim shouldn't have sole responsibility over the company funds. I've invested a sizeable amount of money in New Radiance, and I intend seeing a return on it. If I've got to spend time getting the company on its feet for you then I'd have done better to have invested the money elsewhere.'

'You'll get your precious return, don't worry.'

'Not unless you take control I won't.'

It was an expression of confidence in her, but she couldn't feel any glow of pleasure in his words when he was criticising her brother.

'Are you saying you don't put Jim above swindling you?' she asked, her eyes angry.

'I'm saying,' he told her, setting out the terms clearly, 'that if you intend using my money to keep the company afloat, then you've got to take over the accounts.'

'But I've no accounts training,' she pointed out reasonably. 'Jim's the expert. If I take over his job, what's he going to do?'

'Well, let's hope he finds something else.'

'So that's it!' she said heatedly. 'I might have guessed you'd use this as a chance to get him out of the business. You've always had it in for him.'

'Just what qualities does he have to recommend him as a business partner?' Kirk asked caustically. 'He's a

fool, and fools come to the kind of end you'd expect
them to.'

'I'm not doing anything Jim won't agree to,' she
said with loyal determination.

'You'll do what I tell you.'

'Oh, will I?'

He studied her with hard, analytic eyes.

'You will if you intend keeping New Radiance out
of liquidation.'

Imogen looked down and didn't answer. He took
her lack of reply correctly for acquiescence.

'When I come home this evening I'll start going
through the books with you. By the time you've
worked on them with me you'll be ready to take a
more active role in the company decision-making. I've
seen what you've done with what I'll call, for want of
a better term, the glamour side of the business. I want
that sort of expertise applied to the book-keeping.'

Remembering his earlier judgement of her, she was
surprised he should be expressing such confidence in
her now. Kirk didn't hand out accolades. If he said
she'd handled her side of the business well, he meant
it, and coming from a man whose specialisation was
management consultancy, his opinion meant something.

Curiously, the business which had helped drive a
wedge between them became, as Kirk took her through
the principles of corporate finance, a bridge back to a
closer understanding. She couldn't pretend there were
any similarities between when he had first advised her
on business matters and his help now. There weren't.
They were too formal together. She might have been
a trainee in his company. He was too skilled a mentor
not to provide scope for questioning, analysis and
argument, but the margins of their talking-points were
very clearly set. There was no more likelihood of their
conversation veering dangerously to the intimate than

there would have been if she was his assistant at work.

When a problem cropped up with the break-even chart she was working on, she had no hesitation about asking his advice. They were in his study. The table-lamp made the shadows in the room soft and intimate. Kirk moved the chart towards him and, picking up a pen, said,

'You want to draw the line along here. This way you shade in the area that will tell you the number of customers you've got to get in every week before you go into profit.'

'That's not easy. It's a slack time of year at the moment.'

'Yes, but remember that the weeks, say just before Christmas, when you're really busy, are going to balance this out, and also that you've got to use this in conjunction with your cash budget.'

'I don't like to admit this, but I'm not quite sure what that is,' she confided.

His face relaxed into a smile. He pushed his chair back a little and studied her as though she interested him.

'It shows your projected earnings and projected expenditure. From that, you'll see how much money you're likely to have in the future.'

'I *do* know what that is, then,' she said, correcting her earlier statement. 'Jim's showed me projected figures for the company.'

'Has he?' said Kirk with a faint shading of cynicism in his voice.

Imogen didn't take issue with him. She didn't want to break this new mood of understanding between them.

She went back to work shortly before Kirk's Accounting Institute's annual dinner. This time he didn't query her decision. The taxi dropped her off outside the shop. The salon, like the other two shops, reflected her sense of style. The company hadn't folded and it was Kirk who had made its continued existence possible.

Working alongside him was challenging. For the first time she was teaming up with someone whose energy and drive outstripped her own, rather than working exclusively with Jim. She was sorry that, now she was well enough to resume her role in the business, Kirk was relinquishing his control to her. It was good to have him as a backer, but it would have given her greater confidence in the company's future to have had him as an active partner. The thought was disloyal to Jim and she suppressed it. It wasn't Jim's fault if the gambles he'd taken in expanding so rapidly hadn't paid off.

She spent the morning setting up the next month's promotion features and finalising the arrangements for a fashion show of bridal wear being put on at a London hotel. New Radiance was to be responsible for the models' hair and make-up.

She took a short break from catching up with the paperwork for Jackie to cut and style her hair.

'How's it working out between you and your husband?' Jackie asked with friendly interest.

'At the moment, we seem to have called a truce,' Imogen said before admitting, her eyes troubled despite her tone of acceptance, 'but it will come to divorce in the end.'

'Why? Is Kirk hard to live with?' asked Jackie as she feathered Imogen's layered hair back through her fingers.

'No,' Imogen conceded, refusing to give the real reason for the breakdown of her relationship with Kirk. His involvement with Lydia was something she couldn't bring herself to talk about, not even to Jackie who she knew well. Instead she said with partial honesty, 'But there are times when we seem to argue non-stop.'

'I can't imagine that. You're always so reasonable in the shop.'

Imogen smiled a shade wryly.

'Well, obviously Kirk doesn't bring out the best in me,' she said.

Jackie picked up the blow-drier. It was hard to carry on the conversation above its low, insistent whirr. Raising her voice a little, Imogen used the natural break to switch the topic to the salon and the forthcoming fashion show.

Jackie was angling the hand-mirror so that Imogen could approve the style when she heard Jim's voice in a relaxed exchange with the girl on reception.

'Thanks, Jackie, that's lovely,' she said, slipping out of the robe before crossing to the reception desk.

Jim turned as he heard her approach, a spontaneous smile of pleasure lighting his face.

'Hey, it's good to see you,' he began as he enveloped her in a hug. 'Why didn't you tell me you'd be in the shop today?'

'I called you last night but you were out, and anyway, I wanted to surprise you. I've started work again.'

'Are you sure about this?' Jim asked. 'That was a pretty bad smash you were in.'

'I'm a hundred per cent sure,' she said, smiling at him. 'Come on through to my office and I'll make you a cup of coffee. It seems ages since I've seen you.'

'Yes, well, I haven't wanted to call at the house because of Kirk. I see quite enough of him in the course of the business since you accepted that loan from him.'

Imogen didn't say that he also had agreed to the loan. She was too pleased to see him to think of picking up on his remark. They chatted for some time over coffee before Imogen turned the conversation to the business. She knew he wasn't going to like her insisting she intended having a greater share in the running of the company, but now it was something *she* wanted. She wasn't making the assertion solely on Kirk's insistence.

A shade tentatively, and expecting resistance, she began, 'Jim, now that I am back at work, I want things to change.'

'You don't expect me to learn how to cut hair, do you?' Jim asked jokingly.

'Listen, I'm serious,' she said earnestly. 'From now on, I'd like the responsibility spread more evenly between us. It would not only be a challenge for me, but it would take some of the load off you.'

'I'll consult you if you want,' Jim agreed.

'I want to be more than consulted. I want to be involved.' Imogen paused, then said in a slight rush, 'And as a start I want the company cheque-book to be changed so that both our signatures are required for authorisation.'

'You what?' he asked disbelievingly.

'If not, I know you,' she hurried on. 'You'll say you'll involve me and you'll mean to. But after a while you'll forget all about it and we'll go on in the same old way. I've been very glad to rely on you, but Kirk's right, it's time I pulled my weight.'

'So it's Kirk I've got to thank for this!' he snapped, exploding into harassed anger. 'I should never have let you talk me into accepting the loan from him in the first place. I might have guessed he wouldn't stop at just scrutinising the accounts. God, he's a clever bastard!'

'The company was folding, if you remember,' she told him. 'We had no option but to accept the loan *and* any conditions he wanted to attach to it. But that aside, I can't understand why you're so against his having put money into the business. He's very shrewd and very able. In fact, when it comes to business, I've never known him make a faulty judgement.'

'Well, it seems to me,' Jim said heatedly, 'that you scarcely need me in the business any more. As you once said, you've got Mr Midas himself.'

'Of course I need you. It's a family business.'

'Well, I don't think I want any part of it any more.'

'But why?' she demanded, unable to understand his attitude. 'All the time we were running into debt you were the one who kept being optimistic. Even when I was worried sick, you kept saying that we'd be all right, that the company was going through a rough time, but we'd weather it. If you'd wanted to pull out then, or to wind the company up before it was declared insolvent, I could have understood it. But you didn't, and now, when we really are on a more stable footing, you want to pull out. I just don't get it.'

'And I can't explain it,' Jim said tersely, 'but I mean it, Imogen. I'm through with the company. It's time I looked around for something else.'

'Jim, please reconsider,' she begged. 'We've worked together for over three years and we've never had a wrong word.'

He looked away and didn't answer immediately.

'I want to take a break for a couple of days, anyway,' he said after a troubled pause.

'Where?'

'I thought I'd clear off up to North Wales for a bit.' His voice sounded tired, discouraged.

'I was wrong when I said you didn't know how to worry, wasn't I?' she said contritely. 'These last few months with the business—if you're honest, you've found them every bit as much of a strain as I have.'

Surprise gave his eyes an expression of candour, then he said quickly,

'Yes, I suppose that is what's got me down. Anyway, I'll be in touch as soon as I get back and let you know what I've decided about the business.'

'Very well,' she agreed.

He stood up, and the slope of his shoulders gave the impression of despondency.

Imogen wanted to be more involved in the management of the company, but not at the cost of losing Jim. Forgetting her resolution, she said suddenly,

'It's not because of me you want to pull out is it, because I've said I want both our names on the cheque-book?'

Jim gave her a tired smile.

'No, it's not because of you. In fact . . . ' he broke off and then reaffirmed, his voice troubled, despite his assurance, 'this is nothing to do with you.'

CHAPTER NINE

JIM'S uncertainty about carrying on in the business was a background worry that Imogen couldn't entirely push from her mind. Just what had he meant when he'd implied that Kirk was using her in some way to outmanoeuvre him? Kirk had said he would like Jim out of the company. She knew he could be ruthless, and that, coupled with his ability to hold the key cards when it came to business, made her slightly wary of him. Yet if he was setting her up as an unwitting tool against Jim she couldn't see it. She gave the problem up.

Kirk's loan was a complicating factor, not only when it came to managing the business, but also in her relationship with him. It meant that after they were divorced he would not be entirely out of her life. Keeping a tenuous link with him when their marriage was over was going to be harder for her even than the severance of their year's separation. Only by escaping from him entirely had she been able to persuade herself that she was indifferent to him. Seeing him solely in the context of business, with nothing more to form a bond between them than an interest in the company's performance, could only heighten the lonely isolation she felt when she was with him.

Bob Elland and his wife Carleen were arriving from the States in just over a month's time. Imogen assumed that once the Transit International contract was settled Kirk would have no objection to her leaving him as planned, but she didn't broach the subject. Neither did he.

The evening of the Accounting Institute's dinner he came home early. When they had first been married Imogen had liked the way he had involved her in his life. It was different now. Tonight at the dinner she would feel at best, an outsider, and at worst, a masquerader. They would appear as a couple when, in fact, they were no better than strangers still legally joined together, the emotion in their relationship played out, leaving only a formal courtesy between them. Implicit in the meaning of a masquerade was the fact that it had to end. Maybe that was what she found the most difficult to accept, the knowledge that the evening was a prelude to their final break-up.

She wondered if Lydia would be at the dinner and then, with a sense of relief, realised it was unlikely. As a cost accountant, Lydia wouldn't be attending a chartered accountants' dinner dance unless Kirk had specifically invited her, and as this was a run-through before the Transit International contract, he wouldn't want to make waves.

She ran her bath. Before the accident she had been adamant that she wanted a divorce, that she had to be free from Kirk. When she had first come back, Lydia and the threatening, charged atmosphere had made her determined that, as soon as she could, she'd leave him. So what had changed? Was the thought of their arriving at the dinner dance as a couple enough to make her mawkishly sentimental? Because that was all her feelings amounted to. The inner reproof worked until she looked at her wedding-ring on her wet hand and thought of taking it off, and then the pain that caught at her heart couldn't be confused with sentimentality any more.

For the evening, she had decided to wear an after-six dress in sapphire duchesse satin. She hung it outside the wardrobe, then went over to the dressing-table to look out the platinum pendant ear-rings and necklace she intended wearing. She was about to fasten her blue-shaded stockings when there was a cursory knock at the door. Assuming it was Jeanne, she glanced up as the door opened. Instead it was Kirk who came into her bedroom.

Seeing her, he checked what he had been about to say. In the expressive, charged silence Imogen felt her heartbeat quicken betrayingly as his eyes travelled over her slimness. Her matching bra and briefs in their soft lingerie colours were no more skimpy than a bikini. It was the way he looked at her that made her feel unprotected, vulnerable.

She had thought that the latent sexual tension between them had finally been rendered harmless. For the short interlude that their relationship had been tranquil she had been misled into thinking that she was safe from him physically, if not emotionally. Now, as his eyes took in the youthful tautness of her body, making her shatteringly conscious of her femininity, she realised her defences had only seemed strong because he had chosen not to test them.

She knew she should say something, break the dangerous intimacy of the moment, but before she could, he came towards her. She breathed his name in an unsteady protest as he slid his hands round her waist, her heart lurching at the physical contact.

'Do you have any idea of how lovely you are?' he said, his voice quiet and intense.

He bent to kiss her throat and a giddy sensation of pleasure echoed through her. She fought against it. She had already learned that their relationship needed something more solid than fiery eroticism to make it enduring. His affair with Lydia proved that he took the physical side of their marriage far more lightly than she ever could.

Putting a resisting hand against his chest, she said, her words a shade rushed,

'Let me get dressed. We have to be at the hotel by eight.'

Kirk imprisoned her hand in his own, ignoring her protest. For an instant his dark eyes probed hers and then, as she made to pull away, he tilted her head back with determined fingers, his mouth finding hers. Colours rainbowed behind her closed eyes as she felt his lips part hers. The rough texture of his sleeve was a harsh caress against her bare skin as he held her tightly to him.

He kissed her demandingly and relentlessly, moulding her body to him. Her defiance was swept away in a treacherous need to feel his hard, muscular build throughout every inch of her, to feel him kissing her closely.

As her arms suddenly tightened around his neck and her lips answered his, his mouth became more gentle. When at last he released her, she wasn't sure she could stand without swaying.

'I came in for my cuff-links,' he said, his voice a shade harsh. 'You have a way of distracting me.'

Imogen stepped back hurriedly, picking up her wrap that lay on the bed and slipping it on. Sashing it with slightly unsteady fingers, she said coldly,

'I see myself as something more than a diversion, but perhaps that's how you view all women.'

He came closer to her, his dark eyes mocking her show of chilly composure. With a swift movement he undid the sash of her robe, sliding a hand beneath it as he drawled,

'Well, you're certainly more entertaining than most!'

The bed was behind her, making it impossible for her to draw back. He was hemming her in, not just by his hard, lean build, but by his possessive touch that made her afraid to analyse the swift, turbulent feelings he was arousing in her. Her eyes, stormy and intense, met his and then, as though sensing her distress, he ran his fingers caressingly along her face and said,

'You needn't worry. I never hurry anything that I enjoy, and especially not a woman.'

As he was the Institute's treasurer, it was important that they arrive at the dinner dance on time. His implication that, had it not been for such a commitment, he had intended making love to her perturbed her, making the evening ahead treacherous with possibilities, for the dance would end and they would come home together with the dangerous physical attraction between them still unresolved.

To convince herself of her invulnerability she said hotly,

'I'm never going to sleep with you!'

Kirk didn't contradict what she said, but his eyes challenged her apparent certainty. She was conscious that she was blushing. He kept his gaze on her for an instant longer before saying briefly,

'We ought to be off in about half an hour.'

He fetched his cuff-links and left the room. Imogen sat down on the bed. Her skin still retained in memory the warm pressure of his touch, and she rubbed her arms as though, by doing so, she could destroy the magic. If only physical closeness could have rekindled the rapport they had once had. She was almost tempted to risk that it might. She dismissed the notion and started to dress.

The sapphire dress with its flaring skirt had a subtlety and elegance that suited her. She fastened her platinum ear-rings, then paused to look with faintly troubled eyes at her reflection. Kirk was never going to love her. Why didn't she just accept reality?

Picking up her clutch-bag and throwing her gossamer-fine stole over her arm, she went downstairs. Kirk, arrestingly urbane in white shirt and dinner-jacket, was in the lounge glancing through the evening paper. She had forgotten how the precision tailoring, with its razor-sharp lapels and cuffs and the austere darkness of the cloth, gave an impression of hidden strengths, of an edge of fierceness dormant behind the façade of suavity. It unsettled her.

'I'm ready,' she informed him.

He laid the paper aside, studying her appraisingly.

'You look most beguiling,' he said, his choice of words deliberate.

She didn't need reminding that he found her attractive and that her resistance to him to date was a challenge that interested him.

The dinner dance was being held at one of the large hotels on the outskirts of London. Kirk parked the car and together they went into the bar. After their separation Imogen felt a little uncomfortable at meeting his friends and business associates again.

The first part of the evening was the worst. Kirk stayed by her side until official duties claimed him, the ease with which he re-introduced her to his set suggesting she might only have been away on a business trip for a short spell, instead of being estranged from him for almost a year. They really were giving a most convincing impression, she thought, a shade miserably, of two people who had completely reconciled their differences. How could anyone guess that she was here as a preliminary to a marketing campaign aimed to secure a business contract?

She sensed him watching her approvingly and met his eyes with a slight touch of defiance as he silently applauded her ability to handle the situation. The dinner itself was not quite the ordeal she had expected, for their table included Stephen Kendall, an old university friend of Kirk's, and his wife, Miriam, with whom she had always got on well. For the first time in some while, her head began to throb faintly. It was a strain trying to keep the reality of her marriage separate from the illusion.

The speeches and toasts over, the dancing began. Imogen danced first with Stephen. It was not till later that Kirk partnered her.

She preceded him through the tables. As he took her in his arms he asked unexpectedly,

'When was the last time we danced together?'

'I don't remember,' she said briefly.

Imogen knew if she thought back she could remember, but she didn't want to. The parody of normality was already shortening her temper, and the seduction of the music and the settings was making her conscious of a dangerous cross-current of emotions that drained away her independence even as she strove to maintain it. She saw Kirk smile without humour at her reply as he drew her closer.

The orchestra was playing a selection of slow, haunting theme tunes from some of the more recent film classics. The plaintive melody and slow, sensual rhythm seemed a further conspiracy against her. The dance-floor was quite crowded, yet the other couples, the opulent colours of the women's dresses bright among the dark dinner-jackets of their escorts, scarcely impinged on her senses. She was conscious only of Kirk and the music that seemed to be drawing them together so they were enfolded in a unity of movement. Dancing with him, she thought hazily, was like making love with him. It was discovering a perfect completeness. The thought startled her and she came back to reality to realise she had relaxed against him, her body pliant and unresisting.

The music stopped and she took a definite step back from him as she joined in the clapping. As they returned to their now empty table he caught hold of her by the arm, forcing her to face him.

'Why is it,' he asked, his dark eyes compelling hers,

'that at times I have the strongest suspicion that you're afraid of me?'

'That's absurd,' she protested, angry to find she sounded agitated. 'Why should I be?'

'I don't know,' he said, studying her assessingly, as though he discounted entirely her fierce disclaimer, 'but maybe when we get home we can arrive at some answers.'

With Kirk being one of the Institute's key officials, they were unable to leave until the dance had wound down. They stood talking for a while to the chairman and his wife, the two men discussing briefly the conference that was coming up.

But the semblance of being a couple faded with dismaying speed as soon as they left the hotel and were alone again. They crossed the deserted car park together in silence. As they neared the Mercedes, Kirk said casually,

'The roads will be empty this time of night. Why don't you drive?'

'No,' said Imogen hurriedly. 'I haven't driven since the accident. I can't.'

He opened the door to the driving seat for her and dropped the keys into her hand.

'With three salons, you have to be able to drive,' he reminded her. 'You're not going to want to rely on me for transport for ever.'

His last remark was uncaring enough to give her a measure of transitory courage. Apprehensively, she slid behind the wheel. She waited till he got into the passenger seat alongside her and then said in a rush, the memory of the crash returning with tormenting vividness,

'No, Kirk, I can't drive. I don't want to.'

She wished she could refuse for a more solid reason than a complete inability to master an instinctive fear. But there wasn't one, as, apart from the toasts, she'd stuck to soft drinks all evening. Kirk leaned back in the passenger seat, the shadows of the car interior making the strong lines of his face seem more uncompromising.

'How much longer are you going to dodge everything that frightens you?' he asked quietly.

The parallel with his earlier remark made denial essential. She masked her fear with resentment against him as she started the engine. Kirk didn't distract her by talking, and paradoxically, his presence alongside her gave her the reassurance she needed.

'You're doing fine,' he told her as she approached the junction on to the main road. 'Do you want me to take over when we get to the dual carriageway?'

'No,' she said, her voice taut. 'I'll drive the whole way.'

He leaned forward and switched the car radio on. His relaxed ease was already communicating itself to her, his confidence in her damping down her apprehension.

By the time they reached the house some of her alarm at being at the wheel again had subsided. She turned into the drive, switched off the engine and gave an audible sigh of relief, realising from how shaky she felt just how tense she had been.

As she unfastened her seat-belt Kirk caught hold of her hand, enclosing it in his warm, vital grasp.

'It won't seem so traumatic the next time,' he said gently.

His understanding, in view of his harshness earlier, was unexpected. Her eyes met his for a long moment, then she smiled at him and admitted a shade uncertainly, 'I wouldn't have managed that without you.'

He raised her hand to his lips and the tenderness of the gesture completed his systematic dismantling of her defences.

The house was completely in darkness; Jeanne would

have gone to bed several hours ago. Kirk opened the
front door and Imogen went ahead of him into the
hall. After the shadow-washed streets, the electric light
seemed garish, making her flinch slightly from the
brightness and press her hand to the left of her temple.
Kirk drew her to him.

'Headache?' he asked.

She nodded and said,

'It came on earlier and then eased off for a while.'

'You'd better get some sleep,' he said. 'We'll talk in
the morning.'

Imogen had forgotten that he had said he wanted
some answers from her regarding their relationship.
He had no right to demand any explanation from her
when they were only weeks away from splitting up,
but she wasn't going to state her opposition to him
now. Tomorrow she'd feel better able to stand up to
him.

She took a couple of pain-killers, undressed slowly
and slipped on her nightgown. Her headache had
intensified and she lay for a while in the darkness,
trying not to think of Kirk. Gradually, she felt the
tablets take effect, making her relax into drowsiness.

She was scarcely conscious of having slept when she
woke from the recurrent nightmare with a violent
start. She was cold and shaken and she sat up, trying
to subdue the emotion that tightened her throat. But
the heartbreak and terror of the nightmare only seemed
emphasised by the utter stillness of the night. Throwing
the covers aside, she got swiftly out of bed. She needed
the comfort of Kirk's arms, the reassurance of him
holding her close.

Unthinking of the consequences, she went on to the
landing and into his room. For an instant she stood
just inside the door. Kirk was asleep. She noted the
swarthy curve of his chest, his strong shoulders. He
lay completely relaxed, one hand resting on the bed.

His hands were so sure and capable, hands that knew how to caress and protect.

Seeing him steadied her a little. She pressed her back against the wall and brushed her fingers across her cheek that was wet with tears. The nightmare was receding, making her presence in his room seem needlessly rash. As she edged quietly to the door his voice startled her.

'Imogen?'

He pushed back the duvet and got out of the bed, and she caught her breath at the power of his naked male body. She knew what she was inviting being here in his room, for there was only one interpretation he could possibly give to her coming to him. Yet she seemed unable to move away as he came towards her.

'I've wanted you so much,' he said huskily as he stood looking down at her, his hands caressing the slope of her shoulders.

She shuddered at his touch, conscious of the fierce sensual pleasure of surrender. Her eyes, lost and intense, met his. Her resolutions not to give into him counted for nothing. There was only now and the turbulent emotion he was arousing in her.

His arms went round her and he kissed her with an urgency that made her press her body compliantly, invitingly against his. His firm lips and strong, caressing hands were leading her into a labyrinth of pleasure she would know no escape from till he set her free. When at last he raised his lips from hers she was trembling, her breathing as altered as his.

Deftly his hands slipped the ribbon-thin straps from her shoulders and she felt the soft caress of chiffon as her nightgown slipped with a whisper to the floor. He kissed her again, the firmness of his lips parting her own, and his hard, male body against hers making her respond to him with an abandoned, answering need that half frightened her. A leaping reckless excitement coursed through her as he kissed her deeply, as though appeasing a mutual hunger that had lasted for an eternity instead of twelve empty months.

She gave a faint moan of pleasure as he pressed his lips to her throat, the smoothness of her shoulders and the swell of her breasts. His hands caressed the freedom of her body so that she gloried in her femininity. He pushed her down on the bed, tendering pleasure upon pleasure, ravishing her senses with his insistent caresses. She was losing herself in a tumultuous sea of passion as he swept her with him towards some ever-gathering crest. In the time their marriage had been strong, she had lost her timidity of exploring his body. She cried out, feeling herself approaching a transcending summit. She sensed that his pleasure was as fierce as her own, and even in the surpassing, mounting torrent she rejoiced that she should be the one to give him this overmastering delight.

Then the surging crest reached its tumultuous peak and at the cataclysmic moment of unity, the surrender of self was too shatteringly beautiful to be borne and she burst into tempestuous sobs. It seemed as though she was falling, falling from a dizzy height and she felt Kirk draw her to him so that she could lie against him, her head against his chest.

She needed the protection of his arms and his tenderness, for he had overwhelmed her completely. The widening ripples of response faded slowly from her body and a sense of wonder and quiet joy filled her, for she had never before been swept to such heights, or wept so uncontrollably at the perfection of physical completion with him. And in the sudden profound peace between them, with her senses wrapped in the glow of fulfilment, she said softly,

'You make me feel so beautiful.'

'You never cried that way before,' he said gently, smoothing her hair.

'I never felt that way before,' she told him, marvelling. 'Never.'

He kissed her forehead, his arms holding her close, infinitely tender. Imogen closed her eyes, but she didn't want to sleep. The beauty of the moment when he had possessed her totally, when they had come together in the shattering peak of unity, had left her almost dazed. She felt too utterly at peace to even stir in his arms. Her surrender was recent enough for the merging of herself with him to remain with her senses and she wanted to retain it and not lose it in sleep.

After a while, Kirk's breathing told her that he had drifted into slumber. She moved a little so she could look at his face. Without waking, Kirk slid his arm across her naked waist. She took hold of his hand, pressing it to her heart, her body still recording the memory of the delight of his lovemaking.

It was morning when she awoke. Dreamily, she turned on her side, expecting to feel Kirk's arms encircle her. But the bed was empty, and with a slight start of surprise and disappointment she sat up. She looked disbelievingly at the clock. It was almost ten—no wonder he was not still beside her! Colouring a little at the evidence of how totally at peace his lovemaking had left her, she snuggled down into the sensual warmth of the duvet. He couldn't have been so demanding of her last night, she thought with a surge of happiness, if he felt nothing for her. A new certainty in the strength of their relationship lifted her spirits.

Strangely, the knowledge about her background hadn't altered her perception of herself. She didn't see herself flawed in the way her father did. And remembering the way Kirk had made love to her, suddenly she felt a flickering trust that maybe it wouldn't alter his wanting her as a woman.

Throwing back the covers she got out of bed. She

must phone Jackie to say she wouldn't be in at the shop till later in the morning. She went back to her own room to dress, then went downstairs as the telephone started ringing. Thinking it might be Kirk, she ran down the last few stairs as she went to answer it. But instead it was an unknown woman's voice who spoke.

'Scotts the jeweller's here. May I speak to Mr Cameron?'

'I'm afraid he's out. Can I take a message?' Imogen asked.

'Yes, would you tell him his order's ready? That's the diamond and ruby ear-ring he asked to have made specially.' Imogen's fingers tightened on the receiver, but her voice was perfectly even as she said,

'Yes, I'll tell him. Thank you.'

She put the phone down and stood for a minute in the hall. The bright sunlight still shone thickly on the carpet. The morning was unaltered and yet suddenly it was empty for her.

What a naïve romantic she had been to have believed, even for such a short space, that last night had had any significance for him. He was as involved with Lydia as ever. He was even replacing for her the ear-ring she had lost in his house. The sense of hurt and humiliation intensified. Slowly she walked through into the kitchen and switched on the percolator in an outward pretence that it didn't matter to her that something that had seemed so tender and precious was now tarnished.

Last night had obviously meant nothing to Kirk beyond physical appeasement and a sense of arrogant male victory, and it had meant everything to her. She felt used, degraded. She had given him her whole self freely and lovingly, when she would only ever be an extra in his life. No one but a woman could understand the hurt of realising he had only valued her for the transitory pleasure her body had given him.

She decided abruptly she didn't want the coffee. She went into the lounge where Jeanne was coiling the flex of the Hoover.

'Jeanne,' Imogen began, her voice a shade constrained, 'when Kirk comes in, would you tell him his order's ready at the jewellers? I shan't be home till late.'

'What time would you like dinner?' Jeanne asked.

'I shan't be home for dinner this evening, so make it to suit Kirk,' she said, managing a smile, so that her request sounded no more than an arrangement to fit in with her plans for the day.

Instead she was temporising, for until she could hide her feelings behind an impenetrable show of chilly indifference as to what she had allowed to happen between them, she knew she couldn't face him.

Before, when her marriage to Kirk had seemed intolerable, Imogen had used her work to push back the disillusionment and hurt she felt. She used it again now. The new promotions in the beauty salon had been good for trade and the shop was busy.

She arranged with Jackie the details of the stock-check and then, impulsively, she set aside the figures for the month's takings to leaf through the pages of the local directory. She found the number of a car hire company and phoned to arrange the delivery of a car. It would be a while yet before the insurance on her own car, which had been a write-off, was settled. The prospect of driving still made her apprehensive but, as Kirk had pointed out, with three shops to run she had to be mobile.

And apart from her decision being practical, it also had the aim of lessening her dependence on him. It was a small gesture of independence, but it helped her to believe that she could dismiss what had happened between them last night as easily as he could. The car would be delivered the next day. For tonight, she'd get a cab home. She rang through to Kirk's office to leave a message to say she would be working late and that he needn't pick her up.

She was considering a change of products with one of the hair-care reps when one of the girls told her she was wanted on the phone. Leaving Jackie to take over, she took the call at the reception desk. It was Jim.

'Hi,' she began warmly. 'It's good to hear you. How was your holiday?'

'OK,' Jim said tersely, before adding, 'Look, I need to talk to you. Are you very busy in the shop right now?'

'Fairly. I've got one of the reps in, but come round anyway.'

'No,' he said, his voice troubled. 'I don't want to talk to you if we're going to be interrupted every five minutes.'

'Jim, what is it? Is something wrong?'

'Not particularly,' he said, 'but then things aren't exactly great, either.'

'You haven't decided to pull out of the company, have you?' she asked before going on hurriedly, 'Because listen, we can sort something out about the decision-making.'

There was a short silence, before Jim said, 'I don't know what I'm going to do. That's why I need to see you.'

'Then come round about seven. I'll still be here.'

'OK then,' he agreed. 'I'll see you then.'

Imogen heard him put the phone down and, slightly surprised by his unusual abruptness, she replaced the receiver and went back to work.

CHAPTER TEN

THAT evening, Imogen was the last to leave the shop. She spun out the last few tasks of the day. The salon seemed very still, devoid of the customers' talk with the stylists and the constant whirr of the driers.

She sorted the brushes into their correct containers, then glanced up at the sound of a key in the lock.

'I'm later than I meant to be,' Jim began as he came in. 'The traffic was bad.'

'That's all right, I'm not in any rush,' said Imogen, before asking, 'Would you like a cup of coffee?'

'No,' Jim said a shade abstractedly.

He sat down on the banquette by the reception desk and Imogen joined him.

'What's the matter?' she asked. 'You sounded really bothered on the phone.'

He leaned forward, rubbing his hands together and frowning slightly before looking up and saying abruptly,

'I've made up my mind. I'm pulling out of the company.'

'Oh, Jim, no!' she exclaimed in concern. 'You can't mean it! We've built New Radiance up together. You can't pull out!'

'Look,' he said decidedly, 'there's no point in your trying to talk me out of it, because my mind's made up.'

'But what are you going to do? You could be some time finding another job.'

'That's my business,' he said shortly.

'Well, I only asked,' she said.

He cut across her.

'That means I want my stake in the business back.'

'This isn't the best time to ask for it.'

'Is that why you're so reluctant for me to pull out?'

'You know that's not true,' she protested.

'OK then, if that's not the case, I want my stake in the company back before the month's out.'

'But that's impossible. I can't raise the money that quickly.'

'Don't you understand?' he snapped. 'I need the money now.'

'Jim, you're not being reasonable,' she said angrily.

'Get your damned husband to put the money in,' Jim retorted as he stood up to confront her. 'He's got so much he won't miss it.'

'I'm not asking Kirk for the money,' she said emphatically. 'I'm in debt to him enough as it is. I can pay you out myself, but I need time.'

'You don't understand!' her brother exploded. 'I need that money now. Kirk's got it and he'll have to come up with it. I can't stand the strain of things any more!'

'The strain of what?' she asked. 'We're doing all right now. We're over the worst.'

He studied her for a disbelieving instant.

'Can you really not know?' he demanded despairingly. 'Why do you think the company got into such a mess?' She shook her head in bewilderment and he went on, 'Because I've been milking it for money. I've collected such gambling debts the only way to keep paying off the interest was to draw the money off the company. Ever since Kirk put the money in and started checking the balance sheets I've been terrified he'd tell you what's been going on. God know's why he hasn't, because he knows all right. No tricks with the figures would fool him.'

He broke off and turned away, and the agony in

his face moved her to instant forgiveness.

'How much money do you need to keep up the interest repayments?' Imogen asked with more strength and self-possession than she thought she was capable of.

Jim looked at her in incredulity.

'Don't you realise what I've done?' he said. 'I've been cheating you. I thought I could fix things, pay the money back and you'd never know, but the debts got too large. I almost finished the company for you.'

'That's how you came to tell me the truth about Dad, isn't it, that day at the hospital?'

Jim nodded.

It was some time before he left.

'Try not to despise me too much,' he said, as he paused with his hand on the latch.

'You know I don't,' Imogen said swiftly. 'Jim, I know this has to be the end of your involvement with the company, but I don't want it to come between us.'

'How can it not?' he asked, his tone hollow.

There wasn't an answer. There was a brief, empty silence, then she went towards him. Jim let her hug him before he turned and walked out of the shop.

Slowly, Imogen walked through to her office to fetch her jacket. However much she wanted to, she couldn't delay going home any longer. She was picking up the phone to order a cab when she heard the shop door open. Replacing the receiver, she went back into the beauty salon—then stopped abruptly as she saw Kirk.

She had thought she had her emotions in check, but seeing him made distress rise like a banked tide in her heart. She remembered the way he'd made love to her, the feelings he'd aroused in her. She remembered Lydia.

'Didn't you get my message?' she asked, striving to

keep her voice even. 'I rang your office to say I'd get a cab home tonight.'

'What are you playing at?' he demanded.

'I'm not playing at anything,' she said, dropping her gaze.

He came towards her and asked, his tone kinder,

'What's wrong? You seem upset.'

'Nothing,' she said swiftly, turning her head away, before saying, 'Jim's pulling out of the company.'

Kirk strolled over to perch negligently on one of the stools.

'That's scarcely a tragedy,' he pointed out with faint irony.

'Why? Because he's dishonest?' she asked challengingly, almost glad that he had given her something concrete to fight him over. Antagonism pushed back a little the misery and loneliness of knowing there was nothing left in their relationship. 'You set me up nicely there, didn't you?' she swept on accusingly. 'You knew that if you forced me to get more involved with the company finances Jim would pull out.'

'That, or stop defrauding the company,' Kirk agreed bluntly. 'You may not object to Jim swindling you, but when it's my money that's involved, I object most strongly.'

'You used me!' she said, her eyes angry.

Kirk came towards her swiftly, taking hold of her insistently by the shoulders.

'Stop being a fool,' he told her. 'How did you expect this to work out? Jim had a choice. He could have worked with you, but to do so he'd have had to stop milking the company of funds. He's decided to quit and you're well rid of him.'

'You don't understand,' she said flatly.

'You're damned right I don't understand. I'm not the enemy, so just what is it we're arguing about? Last night . . . '

'Last night should never have happened,' she cut across him, her voice unsteady.

There was a short silence while his eyes raked her.

'Are you going to explain why not?' he asked, his voice dangerously quiet.

'I don't have to explain anything to you,' Imogen said coldly.

He dropped his hands to her waist, sliding his fingers beneath her blouse as though he had a right to her body.

'I think you do. You wanted sex badly last night when you came to my room, and I wanted it too, so why has remorse set in?'

'Stop it!' she exclaimed, her voice unsteady with its vehemence as she pushed her hands against him, his fingers warm on her naked skin when he felt so little for her an affront.

'That wasn't what you said last night,' he reminded her.

His closeness was sapping her will to fight him. In sudden desperation she said,

'I woke up from that nightmare I've had ever since the crash. I was lonely and I needed someone.'

'So you dreamt about Graeme and then came to see me.'

She had forgotten she had made out it was Graeme who featured in her nightmare.

'Yes,' she said, lifting her chin and meeting his gaze with stormy eyes.

'So that explains your reaction last night,' he said bitterly. 'I'd wondered why it had seemed so good.'

'I'm surprised you bothered to think about it at all,' she said, retaliating in a torment of heartbreak. 'Don't tell me Lydia's lost her appeal.'

Kirk didn't answer immediately and then he said, his voice as hard and dispassionate as his eyes,

'You're a much hotter number than Lydia, and in

any case, last night she wasn't available. You were. Despite the glacial act, you're still one of the most responsive women I've ever slept with. Curious, isn't it, to think that after a few weeks together I can still seduce you when Graeme never scored with you in a lifetime?'

She looked away, alarmed by the perceptiveness of his comment, but he caught hold of her by the arm, forcing her to face him.

'What's wrong with you,' he demanded with sudden anger, 'that after all this time you're still tied to a ghost?'

'Leave me alone! I don't want to talk about this.'

'That's your answer to everything. Did it never occur to you that maybe that's why our marriage broke up? I've never met anyone like you for putting up such emotional barriers. For the first time over the last few weeks you'd started to open up with me. Even if we were rowing at least you were saying what you were thinking.'

'Why should I be open with you? There's nothing between us.'

'And yet you've never slept with another man.'

He was getting too close to the truth. Imogen said abruptly, suddenly decided,

'I tell you I'm through with the arrangement we had.'

'You're not a very reliable person to do business with, are you?' Kirk said harshly, tilting her chin towards him. 'I can push you into insolvency tomorrow.'

She pulled away from him sharply. There was a short, brittle silence. She knew better than to think of defying him. It was always safer to be Kirk's partner than his opponent. She'd already learned that.

'All right, then,' she conceded. 'I'll stay with you till the contract's signed.'

'You don't have any choice,' he pointed out. 'Now get your things. We're going home.'

They drove home in silence for the most part. An attempt at conversation seemed useless. She felt Kirk's narrowed eyes stab a thoughtful glance at her as he said with his usual matter-of-fact directness,

'With Jim pulling out, you can't continue with the business in its present form unless you can find someone to replace him as a director.'

She hadn't yet considered this implication of Jim's decision.

'He's not pulling out immediately,' she said, her voice troubled, for the company had too many debts for her to consider New Radiance losing its limited liability status.

'Perhaps we can come to an agreement on it.'

'You mean you'd come in with me?' she asked.

'It's an option. As I've said, I don't want to get involved in the day-to-day running of the company.' He flickered a glance at her. 'But it seems quite an expedient solution. Anyway, think it over. I'm leaving Thursday morning for a business trip to Hamburg. You can tell me your decision when I come back.'

'How long will you be gone?'

'Three weeks.'

At one time he would have asked her to go with him, but undoubtedly, on this trip he would have all the female company he'd need. Lydia was still with his firm and undoubtedly the arrangement was that she would be both working and sleeping with him. Not even when New Radiance had been folding had Imogen felt so utterly defeated.

The three weeks that Kirk was away gave Imogen time to sort out her plans. With their relationship so completely over, there could be no risk in accepting his offer to act as a director with her. The pattern of her days mirrored with predictable accuracy the ones shortly before she had walked out on him over a year ago. She worked long hours. There didn't seem much point in coming home early. The lonely evenings made her only too aware that, no matter how much she tried to deny the idea, she missed Kirk's company.

She called in at her flat a couple of times, in readiness for when she moved back. Possibly, in view of the accident, she was working too hard. She convinced herself that once she had started divorce proceedings, her feelings for Kirk would be severed as completely as her legal ties to him. The strain of living with him again and refusing to acknowledge how deeply she felt about him made her restless. She wanted the Transit International contract to be signed, her obligation to be over, and to be free.

The evening before Kirk was due back she got home late. The fierce September afternoon sunlight had waned, leaving the evening pleasantly warm. Jeanne was in the kitchen listening to an English language cassette and repeating the phrases in the specially provided pauses in a serious voice, full of concentration. She coloured a little and switched the tape recorder off as Imogen came in.

'I was practising my English,' she explained.

'It sounded very good,' Imogen assured her. 'In fact, you're a lot more fluent than when you came here.'

'You really think so?' Jeanne asked, obviously pleased.

'Yes, I do.'

'Would it be all right if we eat in about half an hour?' asked Jeanne. 'I've been asked by some friends to go to the cinema.'

'Yes, that's fine,' Imogen said, going to the fridge for some mineral water.

She stooped down and then, as she got up, the bottle in her hand, she sat down quickly on the nearest chair.

'What is it, Mrs Cameron?' Jeanne asked anxiously. 'Are you all right?'

Imogen drew a deep breath and said with a relieved smile,

'I just felt a bit dizzy for a minute, but it's passed. I've had quite a hard day. Perhaps I've overdone it a little.' She stood up and fetched a glass.

'You don't think . . . ' Jeanne began hesitantly, her voice a shade excited.

'I don't think what?'

'Well,' Jeanne said tentatively, 'you've been wanting a baby for a long time, and women often feel faint . . . '

Imogen stared at her in shocked silence.

'Oh, God,' she said hollowly.

Jeanne mistook Imogen's horror for stunned delight. 'Do you think it might be?' she asked.

The memory of the night of the dinner dance and of her impassioned lovemaking with Kirk crowded in on Imogen and she coloured hotly at the recollection of it.

'No,' she said weakly, denying the suggestion. 'No, it can't be.'

She wanted to check the calendar, but she wouldn't with Jeanne there. If she really were pregnant she needed to make the discovery by herself.

'Jeanne, look, don't bother to cook anything for me,' she said quickly. 'I'll have something later.'

She couldn't be pregnant. She couldn't. There was no way she could manage on her own if she were. She ran upstairs in a frenzy of alarm, trying to calm herself. Of course she hadn't conceived that night. Her illness alone was enough to upset her body rhythms. There was a diary in her dressing-table drawer. She snatched it up, turning the pages, counting the weeks. And then she stopped, shutting it and holding it tightly closed. She was almost certainly carrying Kirk's child.

She sat down slowly on the bed, shaken by the discovery. Kirk had got her pregnant in one night's uncaring, physical gratification, and suddenly she hated him with a depth of hurt anger as she thought of her child growing up, as she had done, without a father's love. She bowed her head, refusing to admit how much she needed Kirk's protectiveness. She was pregnant and utterly alone. She threw herself down on the bed and, pressing her face into the pillow, began to cry silently and without hope.

Time passed and her thoughts became calmer. She heard Jeanne go out, leaving her in the house alone. Slowly she went downstairs. She didn't want to eat, but that mainstay of all crises, a cup of tea, she could manage that.

Her mind went back to the night when she must have conceived. If Kirk hadn't ruined it by showing her that it had scarcely touched him emotionally, would she be so distraught now? Puzzlement came into her eyes as she remembered how close she had felt to him, lying in his arms after he had made love to her. If she had known then, at that moment, that she had conceived, how would she have felt? Wouldn't she have been glad?

She heard the front door open. Jeanne must have forgotten something. Instead it was Kirk who came into the kitchen. At the sight of him, all her anger returned.

'What are you doing here?' she asked curtly. 'I didn't expect you till tomorrow.'

'I took an early flight to be with my charming wife,' he said with light irony.

In a little over a week's time she was leaving him, and now, if she was pregnant, everything was complicated. She turned away, an expression of pain in her eyes.

'What's wrong?' he asked. 'Another headache?'

'Another headache?' she repeated, her voice rising sharply as she got swiftly to her feet. 'I only wish it were!'

'What do you mean?' he said, taking a step closer.

'I'm pregnant, damn you, that's what I mean!'

She was too upset to see either the surprise or the sudden gentleness that came into his face.

'Are you sure?' he asked.

'Yes, I'm sure. I only wish I weren't. God, how I hate you for this!'

Kirk didn't answer immediately. He turned away, a tautness in his shoulders as he remarked lightly,

'Well, try not to hate the baby. Pretend it's Graeme's.'

'Oh, you bastard!' she sobbed, brushing past him as she went to run from the room.

He caught hold of her by the arm. For an instant he seemed unable to find the words he wanted. Then he said quietly,

'I shouldn't have said that. I know you don't want the baby, but I'll see to it that you get the best care.'

'And how are you going to do that? We're splitting up.'

'You can forget that idea,' he said with muted emphasis. 'You're not leaving me now. You can put your flat on the market as from tomorrow. Did you really think I'd let you go through this pregnancy on your own?'

Imogen pushed his arm away. His last, strangely protective remark made her feel suddenly vulnerable and uncertain. Without answering, she walked out of the room. He didn't follow her and she went into the lounge. She felt curiously calm, but beyond the calmness was a sense of wonder which Kirk's question seemed to have kindled. The miracle of life had happened inside her and her former hurt anger had drained away. He might not love her, but he was going to care about their child. She imagined what it would be like to hold her own baby in her arms, Kirk's baby, and a wave of tenderness went through her. If Kirk had loved her this would have been a time for rejoicing.

She remembered his taunt, *pretend it's Graeme's,* and resentment flared again briefly. She didn't want the child to be any man's but Kirk's. And then, with a sudden blinding illumination, she knew why. She was glad she was pregnant, fiercely glad, because she loved him. That night when she had surrendered to him, she hadn't gone to him for comfort or reassurance, but because she had wanted to give her whole self to him. She had tried to pretend her feelings for him were dead. She had even succeeded at times in persuading herself that she had stopped caring for him over a year ago. But now she was carrying his child and she couldn't pretend any longer. She loved him. She had never, not even in their year's separation, stopped loving him.

She knew she didn't mean anything to him beyond a wife who appeared to be an asset and a woman who was sexually desirable, but it didn't seem to matter with the cruel intensity it had. She was pregnant by him. They couldn't have a child together without his feeling something for her.

She thought of the way she had flung the news at him like an accusation, and she regretted it. But a deepening joy made her suddenly confident that she could put things right between them. She had thought she had nothing with which to retrieve their shattered relationship. But she did. She had the miracle of his child.

CHAPTER ELEVEN

IMOGEN didn't sleep for a long time that night. Her initial chaotic feelings about being pregnant were far less confused now. She was still slightly awed by the thought that she was almost certainly carrying Kirk's child. Before, she had assumed she couldn't fight Lydia. Now, in the happiness of knowing she and Kirk were going to have a baby together, she was certain she could.

With her expecting his child, surely she could make him care for her? What Jim had told her about her father wasn't important any more, for as the mother of Kirk's child she would have a different worth to him.

If only she could go to his room, tell him how she felt about the baby, but she couldn't. Not yet. She'd flung the news at him too bitterly for her to be able to share with him what discovering she was pregnant meant to her now she was calmer.

Her eyes darkened a little as she remembered the night she must have conceived. How could he have made such vital, uninhibited love to her if his feelings for her didn't run deeper than he showed? Restlessly, she put her hands under her head. If he loved her then why did he need Lydia, why was he using her to get the contract he wanted, why until tonight had he been so ready to let her walk out of his life? The weight of evidence was conclusive enough.

She started as there was a light tap at the door and she propped herself up on an elbow as Kirk came in.

'You're not asleep, then,' he began.

'Did you think I would be?' she asked.

Seeing him standing in the shadows of the room, his dark hair slightly tousled, his hands in the pockets of his knee-length robe, made a desolate sense of hopelessness catch at her throat. He was so utterly self-contained. His spare, hard body was matched by an equal ruthlessness of purpose and alertness of mind. She wanted to run to him, to go into his arms, slide her hands between his robe over the strong warmth of his back, to share with him the joy that she was expecting his child.

But her love would mean nothing to him. His emotions were beyond her reach. Perhaps they always would be. It was only because she was expecting his baby that he was insisting that she stay.

He came towards her and sat down on the bed. In the darkness she could not read the expression on his face, but his voice when he spoke was level, a shade flat.

'I know you're upset about being pregnant,' he began.

'I'm getting used to the idea,' she said, her voice a shade taut. 'After all, I won't be the first woman to have an unplanned pregnancy.'

He caught hold of her by the arm.

'Unplanned yes, but not unwanted, not on my part, anyway.'

'You really mean that?' she asked hesitantly, hardly daring to trust the sincerity in his voice.

'I like children. It's not exactly ideal, the timing of it, with our marriage so shaky, but no, I'm not sorry you're pregnant.'

Imogen's eyes met his, seeking honesty and then, looking away, she said, her voice expressionless,

'I suppose you want a son to carry on your consultancy business. I'll try not to disappoint you.'

'Imogen!' he exclaimed in a low, troubled voice as

though her words stung. 'For God's sake, let's try and do something about our marriage. I don't want you to go through this pregnancy hating me.'

'I wanted to do something about our marriage,' she reminded him. 'You can't have forgotten the night of the Institute's dinner. After all, my being pregnant is the very tangible result.'

'That was your attempt to bring us closer, was it?' he said, his voice edged with sarcasm. 'I thought I was a stand-in for your long-dead lover.'

'You've never understood the first thing about me!' she retorted angrily, fighting the flare-up of emotion she felt with heated words.

She broke off, a catch in her voice. Kirk pulled her into his arms and she went into his embrace, turning her face into his broad shoulder. She felt his hand smooth her hair.

'I don't want the fact that you're expecting a baby to drive another wedge between us,' he said levelly.

'Nor do I,' she admitted.

He released her a little before asking,

'Have you been to Dr Mortimer yet?'

'No. I'll make an appointment tomorrow.'

'OK,' he said, before kissing her on the cheek and getting up from the bed. 'Sleep well.'

She smiled faintly, then said hesitantly as he reached the door,

'Kirk, I didn't mean it earlier, when I said I hated you. I was on edge.'

He studied her a moment as though debating whether to say more, then he nodded curtly and walked from the room.

She got an appointment with the doctor in two days' time. Jackie came in just as she was terminating the call.

'I'm sorry,' she began, 'but I couldn't help but overhear what you were saying. You're not still feeling under the weather?'

'No,' Imogen answered before saying with a smile, 'I think I'm pregnant.'

Jackie came up and hugged her, sensing her quiet elation.

'Congratulations! That's just wonderful. I suppose Kirk's delighted.

'Well, it wasn't planned,' Imogen admitted, 'and I'm afraid I said some things that I shouldn't. But anyway, don't mention it to the girls yet, just in case it's a false alarm.'

'I won't say anything,' Jackie promised.

Imogen spent some time discussing various aspects of the business with Jackie. The company was on a firmer financial footing than it had been at any time in the last eighteen months. Her pregnancy had already brought her closer to Kirk. After the loneliness of the last few weeks, the brightness of the future made her determined not to lose this chance to put things right with him. She wanted to make their relationship strong and caring again.

Last night she had made a tentative attempt at trusting him with her feelings. Somehow, when she was with him, all her resolution seemed to falter. He was right, she was too reticent about sharing her feelings.

Kirk was home earlier than usual. He asked her if she had made an appointment to see the doctor but made no other attempt to communicate with her. Imogen settled down to a quiet and solitary evening. Jeanne had gone out with some friends, and Kirk was working in the study. She switched on the television. Was this the pattern for their marriage—Kirk working in another part of the house while she watched television as if she was completely on her own? How was she ever going to bring any warmth back into their relationship? She loved him and if only he would let her, there was so much she could give him, love, tenderness, laughter, and the ultimate of all gifts, a child.

She wanted to make their marriage work, but as long as he had Lydia in his life, that was never going to be possible. She stood up and went and poured herself a drink. She rarely touched spirits, but tonight, when she was bracing herself to ask Kirk to give Lydia up, she needed the warmth of a glass of brandy.

Kirk came in as she was recorking the bottle.

'You shouldn't be drinking,' he said, coming towards her.

'Don't tell me what I can and can't do,' she said edgily, picking up the glass.

He took it out of her hands and set it down on a side-table.

'What's the matter with you?' he asked fiercely.

There was something in his voice that touched her, a concern that was overlaid with anger.

She went over to the sofa and said,

'I'm as anxious to have a healthy child as you are. If you'd rather I didn't have a drink, then all right, I won't.'

There was a short silence, then Kirk moved to the television set and turned the volume down. He came and sat down beside her, turning her to face him.

'You're not usually this conciliatory,' he remarked.

'I don't want us to keep arguing, and especially not now.'

His eyes searched hers and then he conceded,

'I shouldn't have snapped at you, but you're important to me, and so's the baby. I don't want you taking any risks.'

Imogen thought of his isolated upbringing and realised, wondering why she hadn't seen it before, how important having a family would be to him. The mood between them was fragile. She didn't want to break it by talking of Lydia now, but she did want to restore their marriage. Then she saw there was another way.

'I don't want to take any risks, either,' she began, 'but if the doctor says it's quite safe . . . ' She hesitated and then continued, feeling the hot colour rise to her face. 'If we're going to stay together, we have to get things better between us. What we've got at the moment is a sham of a marriage. We don't even share a bedroom.'

'Have I got this straight?' asked Kirk questioningly, with his usual cut-through directness. 'Are you saying that you're willing to start sleeping with me again?'

'If it's quite safe,' she said unsteadily.

He ran his hand caressingly along the line of her cheek, making her shiver at his touch.

'You're a very complicated woman,' he said, giving her a smile that made it seem almost as if he loved her.

'Aren't all women?' she asked, suddenly at ease with him.

'Maybe,' he agreed, taking her face in his hands and kissing her lightly on the lips. 'But I think you've got the edge on most.'

With a slight, shuddering sigh she went into his arms, turning her head against his deep chest. She could feel his heart beating loudly and there was a tension in his arms that, as she glanced up, she could see reflected in the taut cords of his neck. He put his hand under her chin and their eyes met for a long moment before he kissed her long and closely.

At last he raised his head and drew her back into the crook of his arm. She undid one of the buttons of his shirt and slid her hand over the strong warmth of his chest. He imprisoned it swiftly in his own.

'I thought you said we'd wait till you'd seen Dr

Mortimer,' he said, his resolute voice gently teasing.

Imogen laughed softly, her grey eyes dark and lustrous.

'I just want to feel close to you,' she said, kicking off her shoes as she tucked her legs beside her and snuggled against him.

'Always,' he said, his arms tightening around her.

It was the afternoon following her appointment with Dr Mortimer when the surgery phoned the shop with the result of her test. She wasn't pregnant. Disappointment numbed her.

The belief that she was expecting Kirk's child had been the one thing holding their marriage together, her trump card against Lydia, the sole reason why the truth about her background didn't matter. She remembered Kirk's tenderness over the last couple of days. She couldn't bear the agony of telling him she wasn't pregnant after all.

Jackie came in with some queries. For a while, Imogen clung to the self-deception that the business would act as a focus for her creative energies. She'd get over the bitter disappointment that she wasn't to give Kirk a child.

They discussed the business for a while and then in a lapse in the conversation Imogen said suddenly,

'Jackie, can you hold the fort here for today, and maybe tomorrow as well?'

'Sure,' Jackie agreed, a shade surprised. 'Why?'

Imogen fought to suppress the knot of emotion that caught at her throat and knew she couldn't attempt an explanation.

'I just want to get away,' she managed. 'I'll be in on Monday.'

She drove home. Going upstairs, she hurriedly packed some overnight things. The impersonal loneliness of a hotel wasn't very appealing, but she was desperate for some haven where she could escape from having to tell Kirk face to face that she wasn't pregnant. This way she could contact him later by phone, tell him there was no reason any more for them to be together. She could lessen the devastation of splitting up by taking the first move herself instead of waiting for him to tell her, as he undoubtedly would now, and certainly would if ever he learned the truth about her background.

It suddenly occurred to her that she didn't have to tell him she wasn't pregnant. Her heart quickened with hope as she thought of trying for another baby without his ever knowing that she hadn't conceived that night. But the wild hope faded and sober reality returned quickly. She wouldn't build a relationship with Kirk on a deliberate lie. She wasn't pregnant and he had a right to know. And, in any case, it might be some while before she was lucky enough to conceive with her monthly cycle still not settled down to its normal regularity.

She went downstairs, and as she did so, she thought of the cottage Kirk owned in Gloucestershire. It was a more welcoming temporary refuge than a hotel. She fetched the key to the cottage from his desk, slipped it into her jacket pocket and left the house. It seemed ironic that only the gentle click of the door behind her should record the fact that she was shutting herself out of his life.

The journey took a little over two hours. It was warm in the car with the sun on the windows. The countryside was just tarnishing to the colours of autumn and, in no hurry to arrive, Imogen drove slowly along the twisting lanes.

A gap in the Cotswold stone wall showed a glimpse of lazily rolling fields and meandering river. She dropped down to the low-lying land of the Severn, and passing the church and clustered houses of the village, drove on to the riverbank and their outlying cottage.

With its slate roof and solid walls, it had a mellowness that was accentuated by the rustic prettiness of the autumnal garden. Despite the warmth of the afternoon, Imogen was conscious of the slight chill that belonged to all empty houses as she went inside. Kirk paid someone locally to keep an eye on the place and a fire was laid in the cast-iron grate in the little sitting-room. She stooped down and lit it, cheered by the friendliness of the cottage, with its uneven white walls and comfortable furnishings. She had been right to come here.

Having driven back to the village for some shopping, she soon settled in. The isolation and cosiness of the cottage pleased her, easing temporarily her sense of desolation. She made herself a cup of coffee and sat in the curving bow window, gazing out at the wind-scudded river and the tall, broken-headed grasses that had gone up straggly along its banks.

A fine drizzle had started to fall, bringing the evening on early. The logs in the grate hissed quietly, scenting the room with their faint resinous fragrance. The table-lamp encircled her in its soft pool of light that left the corners gently in shadows. She sat on the sofa, a book lying idly on her lap while she watched the sudden spurts of hungry flame as a log shifted and the orange sparks flew up the blackened chimney.

It was late when there was the sound of a powerful car turning into the wide drive. Imogen glanced up sharply at the crunch of a man's tread on the gravel. Setting the book aside, she walked through the narrow hall as Kirk came in, his collar turned up against the rain.

'What are you doing here?' she began falteringly. 'How did you work out . . . ?'

'Did it never occur to you I might be worried about you?' Kirk asked, cutting across her. 'You said you expected to hear from the surgery this morning.'

She shrugged and turned quickly and preceded him into the sitting-room. He must not know it wouldn't take much for her to give into tears.

'Well, there's no need for you to worry,' she said, her voice controlled but only by the fiercest effort. 'It was a false alarm. I'm not pregnant.'

There was a short silence, then Kirk said, his voice a shade harsh,

'That must be one weight off your mind. I'm surprised you're not celebrating.'

'Celebrating!' she exclaimed, swinging round to face him, her voice tormented by despair. 'I wanted your baby more than I've wanted anything in my whole life, and you can stand there and say . . . '

She broke off and moved away, determined he wouldn't see her distress.

'Imogen.' His voice was gentle, disbelieving, but she stood motionless.

And then his hands were on her shoulders, turning her determinedly to face him, his eyes intently searching hers.

'You wanted a child by me?'

She realised how nearly she had betrayed herself and said defensively,

'Yes, I wanted a baby. It's not so strange, is it?'

He pulled her into his arms and held her close, as though he wanted to protect her for always, and his concern sapped her will to fight him. She relaxed against him and some of the sadness and disappointment eased as she felt the comfort of his closeness.

He released her a little so he could look down at her.

'There's no reason,' he said softly, 'why we shouldn't have a baby if you want one. Not yet perhaps, not till you're really strong, but next year, when you're properly over the accident.'

Her quickened heartbeat brought a rush of becoming colour to her face. His suggestion confused her. When he spoke to her like this, touched her like this, it was all she could do not to tell him she loved him. If she hadn't learned the truth about her father there might yet have been a future for them.

The thought steadied her. Disengaging from his arms, she said hollowly,

'No. It's no use pretending, Kirk. It's over between us.'

'Is it?' he asked challengingly. 'After what you've just told me?'

He shrugged off his coat and threw it carelessly over the back of an armchair before glancing at the hearth and remarking casually,

'It's a long time since I've made love to you in front of a log fire.'

'What are you talking about?' she said in alarm, taking a step back.

'I mean it's not over between us, and you know it,' he said swiftly, pulling her into his arms.

'Kirk, stop it!' Imogen protested breathlessly, aware that he was unzipping her dress as he bent to kiss her.

'Why?' he demanded simply.

She didn't immediately have an answer. His fingers slid warmly against her skin, sending a shiver of weakness through her.

Deftly, his hands drifted across her back, unfastening her bra. Her dress, eased by his skilful fingers, slipped to the floor. Her heart was racing. Things were moving too fast. In a moment she would be lost in a vortex of longing for him.

'Because I'm not what you think,' she said in a rush.

'You're everything I've ever wanted—surely you

know that by now,' Kirk said hoarsely as his lips came down on hers.

He kissed her deeply, moulding her to him. Unthinkingly, she slid insidious hands beneath his jacket as she relaxed to his kiss. The firmness of his lips as they travelled to her throat made reason momentarily drown in a helpless swirl of pleasure. She had the sensation she was falling and she realised, as the warmth of the fire lapped her body, that he had eased her down on to the softness of the rug.

And then the memories of all the barriers between them came back and she pushed ineffectually against him and said,

'I won't be a one-night stand for you.'

Kirk combed his fingers into her hair, his dark, penetrating eyes searching hers as he forced her to meet his gaze.

'I love you,' he said savagely. 'Can't you understand that? Why do you suppose I'm here?'

She heard the sincerity in his voice but for an instant couldn't credit it.

'No,' she said stubbornly, attempting to free herself. 'You only want me because you think I'm an asset to you, and as it turns out I'm not even much of that.'

'So this *is* to do with your father.'

Imogen raised startled eyes to his.

'What are you talking about?' she gasped.

She sat up, chilly with dismay. His hands were gentle and caressing on her shoulders.

'I got the truth out of Jim this evening when I didn't know where you were or why you'd run out on me,' he said quietly. 'Did you really think this could change the way I feel about you, the way I've always felt about you?'

For a moment it was as though he had snatched her out of a chasm of bleak emptiness, and the sudden emblazoning brilliance that lit up her life seemed almost too much to comprehend. She turned to him, her eyes desperately seeking honesty, meeting his.

'You love me?' she said questioningly, almost tentatively.

'Why do you think I married you, refused to let you go, even when I knew you didn't care for me and maybe never would?'

'But you said . . . ' she began, hardly daring to trust what Kirk was telling her.

'I've said a lot of damned fool things to you,' he interrupted with muted force, 'but through it all I've never stopped loving you. I thought you must see it in my face every time I looked at you, however hard I tried to disguise it. Telling you how much I loved you when I knew it was Graeme you still belonged to, heart and soul, seemed like a display of weakness. Arrogant male pride was always in the way. I thought I could fight a shadow and you proved to me constantly I couldn't.' He paused, then turning her palm to his lips, added quietly, 'Until now.'

He felt her resistance ebb and asked, his voice gentle,

'Does finding out about your father matter very much to you?'

She shook her head and said inadequately,

'Not now. Not any more. It did at first. It mattered terribly, but then I realised I could come to terms with the fact. It was only when I thought you wouldn't want me . . . '

She broke off and for an answer he bent his head and kissed her.

'I wish you'd told me,' he said, before smiling at her and adding, 'Where you're concerned I seem to have had to go so much on guesswork. When I realised you'd left me this evening, I kept going over what had happened between us. We'd seemed so much closer, and then I remembered that day you collapsed at work and how upset you'd been, not over the business, but over something to do with your father.'

'I would have told you, but I was so certain you'd hate me for it.'

He kissed her again, gently at first and then with an increasing urgency, his body covering hers as he eased her down on to the soft rug. At last he released her a little, his hands ceasing their exploration of her body.

'Say you're not leaving me,' he demanded. 'I can't go through that hell again.'

He was making her believe the impossible. He loved her, and the future was emblazoned with such possibilities she couldn't think of Lydia.

'For as long as you want me,' she whispered.

'A lifetime,' Kirk corrected her as he kissed her throat.

His demanding hands drifted sensuously across her skin. Only he who knew her body so intimately could bring her so swiftly to this driving need for him. She murmured his name, entreating him to complete the exploration into delight he had started. Every nerve, every muscle, every cell of her body seemed to be aroused by his caressing hands and firm, relentless lips. Her whole being yearned for unity with him. He had taught her a maturity and intensity of response in bed. Love gave an extra dimension.

Afterwards, lying in his arms, she sensed he was as deeply moved as she. Unselfconsciously, she stirred slightly, pressing a series of kisses to his swarthy chest.

'How did you know I was here?' she asked softly.

'Just a hunch,' he said, 'which was confirmed when I saw the key to the cottage had gone from my desk.'

He stroked her hair and, in the tranquil silence, asked,

'This morning when you heard from the surgery, why didn't you call me?'

'I couldn't. I was so certain it meant the end of everything. I thought you'd only wanted me back in the first place because of the contract with Transit International.'

'The contract was signed over six weeks ago,' he informed her.

'But . . . ' she began incomprehendingly.

'You can't really think I wanted you back with me because of a contract?' he queried.

'Oh, Kirk, why didn't you tell me? Why did you let me go on believing you only wanted me because I was useful to you?'

'I couldn't think of any other way to force you into living with me again,' he said, his voice intense. 'You'd told me you were involved with someone else and I was half out of my mind with the thought that I'd already lost you. I'd only let you go in the first place because you so obviously were still in love with Graeme. I thought time might succeed where I'd failed.'

Imogen laid her cheek against his chest, running her hand sensuously over his hard-muscled body as she admitted,

'You didn't fail. You were right when you implied that if I'd loved Graeme we'd have slept together. I realised that in the first year we were married. I've only ever wanted you.'

Kirk turned towards her, pushing her gently on to the rug as he looked down at her and said, a hint of buried laughter behind the exasperation in his voice,

'And you let me believe, when we made love that night, it was Graeme you were thinking of!'

His comment reminded her of the exact reason why she had used that pretext to hide her feelings from him. After the phone call from the jeweller's, she'd assumed he'd wanted her that night solely for her body. He was still involved with Lydia.

Kirk brushed a wisp of hair away from her face with a lightly caressing hand and said fervently,

'God, how I've missed you! If you knew what I went through when you were in the accident, how I blamed myself!'

'But why? A lorry ploughed in on me. The accident had nothing to do with you.'

'I tried to keep telling myself that, but I'd let you drive away knowing I'd upset you. I kept wondering if your reactions might have been just that shade quicker if we hadn't argued.' He broke off, holding her close, the harrowed emotion in his voice making her suddenly want to weep.

'It wasn't you who upset me that morning,' she said, moving her fingers caressingly against his chest as she lifted her head to look at him. She paused and then, before she had time to let hesitation override her decision, she asked with sudden courage, 'I met Lydia at reception. Is it over between you and her? Really over?'

He stabbed a sharp glance at her, as though unprepared for the question in view of the depth and abandon of their lovemaking.

'There was never anything serious between us,' he said levelly. 'And what there was was finished more than a year ago. She's working for another company and has been since you walked out on me. When you called at the office we were involved in consultancy work for them. Lydia stopped by with some papers that morning. I haven't seen her since.'

He was lying to her, and his motive for doing so could only be that his relationship with Lydia wasn't finished. He interpreted her silence correctly as disbelief.

'I never slept with Lydia,' he said, his voice even, 'not even when things were going so badly and I wanted to forget you. When she sent you that hotel bill she was getting back at me. I'd booked a double room, intending that you'd come on the trip with me, but then I realised it was useless. You seemed so tied to Graeme's memory. I suppose I'd got tired of trying to make you feel something for me. Lydia came to my room. She's not very subtle. She offered herself to me and I turned her down. I knew then that I couldn't forget you, however much I wanted to. The same's true now. I don't want any woman in my life, or in my bed, unless it's you. When you accused me I got tired of denying it. I let you think I was involved with Lydia because if you were jealous maybe it showed you weren't completely indifferent to me. But from the time you came into my life, I've never as much as looked at another woman.'

Imogen put her fingers to his lips and said, her voice a shade unsteady despite the soft smile she gave him, 'You don't have to go on. I'd been so cold with you—and anyway, it's all in the past.'

'You think I'm lying to you,' Kirk said slowly, his eyes narrowing as they studied her analytically. 'Why?'

She didn't answer immediately and then she said reluctantly,

'Because I found the ear-ring she dropped in our bedroom.'

Comprehension came into his face followed by a slow amusement of some irony she couldn't see.

'Describe it for me,' he said, before supplying the words for her. 'A diamond set with rubies?'

'Yes,' she agreed stormily.

'No wonder I couldn't work out why you were so changeable with me!' he exclaimed quietly.

She looked at him in faint bewilderment, her jealous anger fading.

'You'll have to have it made into a ring,' he said with a smile. 'You're not going to want three ear-rings.' He touched her cheek lightly as he exclaimed,

'They were a present for you. I bought them in the summer with the idea of them being some kind of token of reconciliation when you said you wanted us to meet and talk. I didn't know then that you intended asking for a divorce, and in any case, the house was burgled before I could give them to you. The neighbourhood watch scheme meant the police were called and the thieves must have been disturbed. The jewellery box, with one ear-ring still in place, had been dropped on the stairs as they got away. Although I looked, I never found the other. I assumed it had gone, so I had another made to match. And even then I didn't give them to you. With the way things were between us I thought you'd see them as a bribe to get you back into my bed.'

'I don't need a bribe for that,' she said.

Kirk drew her close to him.

'I know it was getting that hotel bill from Lydia that made you leave. Things hadn't been good, but that was what broke us up. I handled it all wrong. I should have explained then.'

'If I hadn't been so distant with you, maybe we would have talked it out. I didn't want to be, but somehow I didn't know how to put things right, and then when I got Lydia's letter implying I didn't satisfy you . . .'

'Didn't satisfy me!' he said with swift emphasis. 'I don't know how I've kept my hands off you these last weeks.'

'You didn't, if you remember,' Imogen said laughingly.

She felt his lips brush her hair and she closed her eyes, filled with an infinite contentment. Much as she valued the shared pleasure of their lovemaking, it was this relaxed, uninhibited conversation in the tender afterglow which proved that their union was complete. Not even the climax he had drawn her to the night of the Institute's dinner had had this deeper element to it.

'It's taken a long while to get things right between us, hasn't it?' he said. 'A long time for you to really trust me with your thoughts.'

'The way things were at home, I suppose I got used to keeping my feelings hidden,' she told him. 'I thought you'd taught me about being physically close to a man, but you've taught me so very much more than that.'

There was a long, relaxed silence. She was enveloped by his protectiveness and love. For the first time, she realised there was nothing she couldn't say to him, nothing she couldn't trust him to understand.

'I was going to put the cottage on the market,' Kirk said at last, glancing down at her with a smile that held an amused knowingness, 'but I've a feeling we're going to be spending a lot of weekends here from now on.'

'What makes you think that?' Imogen asked mischievously.

'Because,' he said meaningfully. 'I have a real thing about log fires and we've got a whole long winter to look forward to.'

Her giggle was lost in a swift intake of breath as his courtship of her body began again. The shadows of the fire flickered over the ceiling. Outside the rain struck the glass with persistent faintness, emphasising the stillness that was broken only by the midnight murmurings of love.

Take 4 best-selling love stories FREE

Plus get a FREE surprise gift!

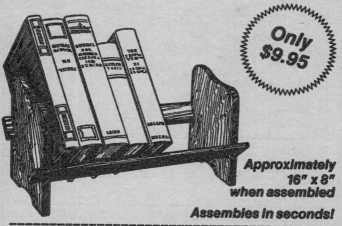

MAIL-IN-OFFER
OFFER CERTIFICATE ✂

002

I have enclosed the required number of proofs of purchase from any specially marked "Gifts From The Heart" Harlequin romance book, plus cash register receipts and a check or money order payable to Harlequin Gifts From The Heart Offer, to cover postage and handling.

CHECK ONE	ITEM	# OF PROOFS OF PURCHASE	POSTAGE & HANDLING FEE
	01 Brass Picture Frame	2	$ 1.00
	02 Heart-Shaped Candle Holders with Candles	3	$ 1.00
	03 Heart-Shaped Keepsake Box	4	$ 1.00
	04 Gold-Plated Heart Pendant	5	$ 1.00
	05 Collectors' Doll Limited quantities available	12	$ 2.75

NAME _____

STREET ADDRESS _____ APT. # _____

CITY _____ STATE _____ ZIP _____

Mail this certificate, designated number of proofs of purchase (inside back page) and check or money order for postage and handling to:

Gifts From The Heart, P.O. Box 4814
Reidsville, N. Carolina 27322-4814

NOTE THIS IMPORTANT OFFER'S TERMS

Requests must be postmarked by May 31, 1988. Only proofs of purchase from specially marked "Gifts From The Heart" Harlequin books will be accepted. This certificate plus cash register receipts and a check or money order to cover postage and handling must accompany your request and may not be reproduced in any manner. Offer void where prohibited, taxed or restricted by law. LIMIT ONE REQUEST PER NAME, FAMILY, GROUP, ORGANIZATION OR ADDRESS. Please allow up to 8 weeks after receipt of order for shipment. Offer only good in the U.S.A. Hurry—Limited quantities of collectors' doll available. Collectors' dolls will be mailed to first 15,000 qualifying submitters. All other submitters will receive 12 free previously unpublished Harlequin books and a postage & handling refund.

OFFER-1RR

PAMELA BROWNING

...is fireworks on the green at the Fourth of July and prayers said around the Thanksgiving table. It is the dream of freedom realized in thousands of small towns across this great nation.

But mostly, the Heartland is its people. People who care about and help one another. People who cherish traditional values and give to their children the greatest gift, the gift of love.

American Romance presents HEARTLAND, an emotional trilogy about people whose memories, hopes and dreams are bound up in the acres they farm.

HEARTLAND ... the story of America.

Don't miss these heartfelt stories: American Romance #237 SIMPLE GIFTS (March), #241 FLY AWAY (April), and #245 HARVEST HOME (May).

HRT-1

GIFTS FROM THE HEART
from *Harlequin*

FREE BY MAIL With proofs of purchase
plus postage and handling

A. Hand-polished solid brass picture frame 1-5/8″ × 1-3/8″ with 2 proofs of purchase.

B. Individually handworked, pair of heart-shaped glass candle holders (2″ diameter), 6″ candles included, with 3 proofs of purchase.

C. Heart-shaped porcelain keepsake box (1″ high) with delicate flower motif with 4 proofs of purchase.

D. Radiant gold-plated heart pendant on 16″ chain with complimentary satin pouch with 5 proofs of purchase.

E. Beautiful collectors' doll with genuine porcelain face, hands and feet, and a charming heart appliqué on dress with 12 proofs of purchase. Limited quantities available. See offer terms.

HERE IS HOW TO GET YOUR FREE GIFTS

Send us the required number of proofs of purchase (below) of specially marked "Gifts From The Heart" Harlequin books and cash register receipts with the Offer Certificate (available in the back pages) properly completed, plus a check or money order (do not send cash) payable to Harlequin Gifts From The Heart Offer. We'll RUSH you your specified gift. Hurry—Limited quantities of collectors' doll available. See offer terms.

103R

GIFTS FROM THE HEART
ONE PROOF
OF PURCHASE

To collect your free gift by mail you must include the necessary number of proofs of purchase with order certificate.